Not Quite Famous

A romantic comedy
of an actress on the edge.

HEATHER SILVIO

Panther Books

Published in the United States by Panther Books, Worldwide.

Correspondence to the author may be sent to:
heather@heathersilvio.com

Cover design by Sonia Freitas at Chloe Belle Arts
https://ChloeBelleArts.com

ISBN (Print) 978-0-9908005-2-1
ISBN (E-book) 978-0-9908005-3-8

In loving memory of my grandmother

BOOKS BY HEATHER SILVIO

PARANORMAL TALENT AGENCY

Lights, Camera, Action (Episode One)

Reset to One (Episode Two)

That's a Wrap (Episode Three)

An Unexpected Sequel (Episode Four)

Jumping the Shark (Episode Five)

The Season Finale (Episode Six)

NON-SERIES FICTION

Not Quite Famous: A Romantic Comedy of an Actress
on the Edge

Beyond the Abyss: Tales of the Supernatural

Courting Death

NONFICTION

Special Snowflake Syndrome: The Unrecognized
Personality Disorder Destroying the World

Happiness by the Numbers: 9 Steps to Authentic
Happiness

Stress Disorders: A Healing Path for PTSD

ACKNOWLEDGMENTS

Thanks as always to my husband, Sidney, for his ongoing support. Thanks also to my "beta" readers, Daniela, Lori, DeLana, and Jeannie!

EAST COAST

CHAPTER ONE

"Hello?"

"Stay away from my husband, you whore!" The line disconnects before I can reply with a witty retort, but, honestly, what could I say?

"Who was that, Gracie?" Jane Romero, my roommate of two years, asks the question, but clearly her interest lies in the dish she's concocting. Like me, she is in her 20s, but the similarities end there. While I define petite at 5'2", 100 pounds, she is taller with a bigger frame. Oh, and my name is actually Graciella Corsini, but everyone calls me Gracie.

"The angry wife," I respond, and that gets her attention.

"The angry wife? What are you talking about?"

"I'm guessing that was the lovely Alicia White," I answer with a sigh. This is not going to end well.

"Alicia who?" Jane is clearly perplexed, but probably because her attention remains half on her cooking. Jane works as a chef and quite frequently delectable scents waft from the tiny kitchen in our two-bedroom midtown Manhattan apartment.

"Christopher's wife."

"I thought they had an open marriage."

"So did I," I reply, already scrolling down to my married boyfriend's work number.

"Christopher White, please," I tell the receptionist at the fitness center who answers.

"Training office. Christopher White speaking."

"Hi, honey, it's Gracie. Your wife called. We need to talk," I tell him before he has a chance to say anything more.

"What?"

I don't respond. You'd think after a few months of dating it might have occurred to him to tell me his wife was not, in fact, accepting of our relationship.

"What did you say?"

"You heard me."

"What…what did she say?" He stammers out the question.

"Um, let me see. She said, *Stay away from my husband, you whore.* Or something to that effect." Crickets chirp on his end, so I continue. "Not the words you expect from a woman in an open relationship." Long seconds of silence pass before he finally speaks.

"What do you want me to say?"

"You lied to me," I respond.

"I know."

"Why?"

"Why do you think?"

"Don't answer a question with a question," I snap, noting the rise in my voice and forcing myself to take a calming breath. "Why did you lie to me?"

"Because I wanted to be with you," he finally answers.

"How original. Be with me or have sex with me?" I ask the question, eyes closed, head tilted toward the ceiling. I never wanted to be *that* woman, the other woman. I hear mumbling on Christopher's end, as though he is covering the receiver with his hand.

"I have to go, Gracie. Can we talk about this later?"

I don't know my answer to that question, so I simply disconnect the call. I'm dismayed to realize I've begun crying.

"Are you okay?" Jane asks, a look of concern on her face.

"I will be."

"What happened?"

"He lied. It was supposed to be a casual, fun relationship. Not just about sex," I hasten to add. "A casual relationship that would be no stress and no pain. And he's turned me into a whore."

"You're not a whore," Jane contradicts immediately to help me feel better.

I grab tissue paper off of the counter. "The funny thing is, I'm fine with the relationship ending. I just feel like such an idiot. I should have known he was lying."

"How could you have known?"

"He's a man, isn't he?"

Jane laughs and, as I blow my nose, I remember our conversation when Christopher and I first met. He never actually said the relationship with his wife was an open one, I realize now, until after I had provided the opening. I vividly recall the day and the conversation…

Oh, how I love hot chocolate on a cold day. Sitting in a coffee shop around the corner from my apartment, enjoying my delectable beverage, I notice an attractive man enter the place. Now, New York City overflows with attractive wannabe actors and actresses. I mean, throw a stick, and you'll hit a dozen. Anyway, he's tall, blond, clearly works out. Kinda looks like a Ken doll — nice eye candy. He notices me watching him and we smile simultaneously. It's his turn at the counter and I watch while he places his order. I continue to watch him as he gets his drink and walks over to my table.

"Is this seat taken?"

"It is if you sit in it."

"That's good." Mr. Ken Doll sits down across from me. "I'm Christopher."

"I'm Gracie." That's when I notice the wedding ring.

"Yes, I'm married."

"You were flirting."

"Au contraire. I had only just begun to flirt."

"Then before we go any further, let me guess. You and your wife have an understanding. Or maybe your wife just doesn't understand you?" I eye him expectantly.

"Which one of those choices results in our having dinner together?"

"Seriously, what's the deal? I'm fine with a casual relationship with someone who's already involved, so long as all parties are okay with it. Do you have an open relationship?"

"Would I be wearing my wedding ring picking up another woman if we didn't?"

"Trying to pick up another woman," I remind him.

"Trying to pick up another woman, then."

"I guess not. At least I'd hope not."

"Does that mean you'll have dinner with me? I'd say now," he hurries, "but I have a client I need to meet." I give him a quizzical look. "I'm a personal trainer." He pauses. "It's a date?"

"Do you know the Thai place two blocks up, on the corner?" Christopher nods yes. "Can you meet me there tomorrow night at 8?"

"I'll be there with bells on. Or maybe I'll leave the bells at home." He smiles and I laugh. "I'll see you tomorrow, Gracie."

"Looking forward to it, Christopher."

The cell phone in my hand rings to life, startling Jane and me. The caller ID reads Christopher-Work.

"Are you going to answer?"

I don't answer Jane's question. I strive for a neutral tone in my voice when I answer the call. "Yes, Christopher?"

"Gracie, please don't hang up on me!"

"I thought you had to go."

"Gracie, please."

"You have three minutes," I say, with as much coldness in my voice as I can muster.

"Okay, listen, I am so sorry that Alicia called you and said…what she said. She had no right to do that."

"This is what you want to say to me," I interrupt him. "You want to blame your wife for catching you cheating and revealing your lie to me? That's a waste of precious seconds." Silence stretches for so long, I begin to wonder if the call dropped.

"Can we meet?"

"Why?"

"I can't–" Christopher stops. I hear a sharp intake of breath. "Please, Gracie, can we discuss this in person? I would appreciate it. I know I don't deserve it."

"No, you don't." This time the silence is mine. Christopher wisely keeps his mouth shut while I decide what to do. I watch Jane vigorously shaking her head no, so I know her feelings. I close my eyes again.

"Tomorrow at 10 at the coffee shop. You know the one. If you're late, I'm leaving." I disconnect the call before he responds. The phone almost immediately starts ringing again, so I turn it off completely. Jane's eyebrows lift in question. I shrug.

"He can talk to me tomorrow."

"Are you sure that's a good idea?"

"No," I say with a sigh and flop down on the couch burying my head in a cushion. I hear the freezer door open and know she is getting out the chocolate-chip cookie dough ice cream. There is a reason ice cream has become the stereotypical comfort food for women.

"What can he possibly say?" Jane hands me a spoon and places the tub of ice cream between us.

"I have no idea," I answer between mouthfuls. "But, maybe I'll want to say something to him."

"What would you want to say to him that you didn't just say?"

"I don't know. Maybe I can just get pissed and throw my latte on him."

"Now that's a plan." Jane starts laughing and it is contagious. Soon, we're both laughing and I pantomime throwing a glass at the liar. "What a jerk."

"Yeah." We eat a few more mouthfuls in silence. Jane looks apologetic. "I know," I begin, "you have to get up early. It's okay. I've got the ice cream."

"Thanks. At least it'll be over tomorrow." Jane rinses off her spoon. "Anyway, good luck."

I wave goodnight to her as she closes her bedroom door.

When my alarm goes off the next morning, I'm uncertain at first why I have such a sick feeling in my stomach. Then, I remember. The feeling stays with me as I go through my morning routine. It intensifies when I arrive at the coffee shop at 9:55 a.m. and find Christopher already at a table waiting for me. At least he took my warning about being on time seriously.

"You look terrible," I tell him, by way of greeting, as I take the other empty seat at the table and place a hand around a cup of water he had obviously already gotten for me.

"Thanks. I thought we could try to be civil about this."

"You're kidding, right?"

"Of course, what was I thinking? Thinking we could act like mature adults."

"Mature adults don't cheat on their wives and lie to others they care about," I remind him. He looks chagrined, but doesn't respond. I sigh. "What did you want to talk about?"

"I wanted to apologize. I never meant for any of this to happen." I must have quite a look on my face, because he hurries to continue. "Once I met you, I couldn't think straight. You are everything I imagine my perfect partner to be." Damn, he's good. I'm actually softening a bit toward him. Not that he has a chance of ever touching me again, but I might not throw my drink on him. Let's see where he goes with this.

"What about your wife?"

"She and I have been married for five years. I didn't lie about that. But, we don't…have an open marriage."

"No, really?" I ask the question, my voice fairly dripping with sarcasm.

"It's your standard story," he starts.

"You mean excuse," I interrupt.

"Please, let me finish."

"Fine, whatever."

"After we got married, we started drifting apart. She stopped getting the higher paying modeling jobs and became a dancer." He paused to sip his coffee. "So, she was working nights and I was working days at the gym."

"Wait a minute," I interrupt again. "A dancer? Is your wife a stripper?"

"Yes, but that's not the point. About two years ago, she began using meth."

"Methamphetamine?"

"Yes," he sounds annoyed at my repeated interruptions. "The last six months have been particularly rough between us. The last months with you have been great."

"Hold up, lover boy. First off, what we *had* the last few months was fun and, let me stress this, *casual.* More importantly, I want to make sure I understand you."

"Of course," Christopher eagerly agrees.

"You lied to your crazy, meth-head stripper wife about me. The same wife who has my phone number and may know where I live?" I may as well have said, "cue the angry wife", because, before he has a chance to retort, a blond-haired, blue-eyed, inflated chest, extremely pissed off woman appears at our table. She presents quite the contrast to my more ethnic Italian American appearance – olive skin, ultra-long curly brown hair and sparkling (or so I've been told) brown eyes.

"Oh, god," Christopher gasps, turning deathly pale.

"You really should have listened to me!" Alicia White yells at me.

"Is that a threat?" I stand up and face her squarely. Her stance doesn't adjust in response and I wonder if she is high right now. Plus, of course, she's waaay taller than I am.

"I don't make threats, only promises."

I have a bad habit of laughing at inappropriate times and this is one of them. "Are you kidding?" I laugh and say to Christopher, "You didn't tell me she was a B-grade actress. That's a great line." As I turn back to face Alicia—

Slap! Holy crap, the bitch slapped me! I don't care if she was the victim of his philandering or not, nobody hits me.

"You need to cool off," I angrily retort with my own B-grade line. I'm staring in her eyes as my fingers blindly grasp for my cup of water and toss it in her face. Watching her anger turn to shock and then back to anger, I have time to register the fact that my water is pretty brown. Yes, I had just thrown Christopher's coffee in her face, instead of my water. Thank goodness, it had cooled some.

"Ladies, please," Christopher pleads with us. "That's enough."

"Yes, it is," I agree. "Christopher, we're finished. Alicia, your husband lied to us both and I realize you're pissed. However. If you ever touch me again…" I trail off. "And that *is* a threat." Before either can respond, I turn and walk from the restaurant. At least it's finally over.

CHAPTER TWO

"Don't you look like the cat that ate the canary," Jane comments after I enter our apartment. With her short blond hair pulled off her face and the most fabulous smell coming from the kitchen, I deduce that she has been experimenting again. This is almost always a good thing.

"Do I?"

"Alright, spill," she orders. She takes a seat on the couch and gestures to the other half. "Sit." The television is on in the background and Jane mutes it.

"Yes, ma'am," I respond, offering a mock salute. "I just spoke to Catherine about a possible job next month. It's a feature length drama."

Yes, I confess – I am an actress. I've always been on the periphery of what the popular culture would consider entertainment success. Okay, waaay on the periphery. I am a professional extra, what's known in the biz as a "background actor". I know what you're thinking, but I pull down a decent living. Plus, I occasionally land a commercial or an "under five" part. That's industry-speak for a bit part where I actually get some lines, usually fewer than five. Those are great because you get a big jump in pay with less work. I realize that when most people think of Hollywood, they think of, well, Hollywood, as in Los Angeles, not New York. But, tons of movies and television shows shoot in the Big Apple, providing a girl like me with plenty to do.

"They don't usually arrange bit parts and extras that far in advance, do they?" Jane interrupts with her question.

"What? No," I am momentarily confused. "That's the point," I continue excitedly.

"It is?" Now Jane looks confused.

"Yes! The casting director saw one of my under-five parts on some TV movie and thinks I'd be perfect for this role in the film."

"What role?"

"It's the part of the lead's former girlfriend who gets murdered. It triggers the whole plot!"

"That sounds great. Wait, it also sounds like a fairly large role. I thought you didn't like more than a few lines."

"That's true," I admit. "There's a reason for that." I hesitate.

"What's going on?"

"It's not that I don't want the lines, actually. It's more that I worry I couldn't do it."

Jane laughs. "You're kidding." She reads the look on my face. "No, I guess not. Why would you think you couldn't do it?" She seems genuinely perplexed.

"Usually, the time from audition to filming is pretty short."

"And?"

"And…I'm severely dyslexic. I need more time to decipher and memorize than that," I say this last in a rush and Jane's eyes widen.

"That's why you never do larger roles?"

"Yeah."

"I wish you had told me. I would have helped you."

"I was embarrassed. Plus, I could never do the cold reading that's usually required in an initial audition for a bigger part."

Understanding dawns in Jane's eyes. "That's the difference this time."

"Absolutely. Filming won't be for a month and I don't have to do a cold reading audition. I've been given the sides already and the audition is in a week, giving me plenty of time." I am completely excited again. If I could see myself in a mirror, I'd probably be glowing.

"That's fantastic. Congratulations," Jane offers warmly.

"Thanks. Who is that?" A face on the television screen catches my eye.

"I don't know, but he's hot." Jane turns the sound back up and we listen to the story.

"Is she or isn't she? Julian McNamara married Lydia Strom after a whirlwind romance on the set of their last film resulted in Lydia becoming in the family way. Only, according to an anonymous source in Julian's camp, the bloom is definitely off the rose now that six months have passed and Lydia doesn't look any bigger." Pictures of an attractive – and quite slender – redhead pop up on the screen, only to be replaced by a photo apparently from their wedding, dramatically cut in half by the show's editors. "Is the romance over for *Heart's Home* breakout star Julian McNamara?" The announcer moves on to a story about yet another drunk pop princess and Jane presses Mute.

"I may have to start watching *Heart's Home*," I proclaim with a chuckle.

"No kidding," Jane agrees. "How is it that soaps always seem to have the hottest men on them?"

"Great place to get started on television and lots of roles to fill," I answer, although I suspect the question was asked rhetorically.

"We'll have to rent his movie. Anyway," Jane changes the subject. "Congrats again on landing the audition. I know you'll do great. If you need any help, just ask."

"Thanks, I will."

Jane stands up as my cell phone rings. I see my mother's picture on the cell phone face and decide I'm not up to chatting with her. After a few moments, the phone chirps that I have a new voice mail message. Apparently she is coordinating a family dinner in a few weeks at my parents' place in Brooklyn, where I was born and raised. Also, I discover I have an unchecked older message from my friend, Renata, wanting to know when I'm visiting Los Angeles. I really need to call her back.

CHAPTER THREE

"What are you doing here?"

"I wanted to talk to you."

"You know I don't like people dropping by my apartment unannounced. Especially people of the ex-boyfriend-who-lied-to-his-meth-addict-wife variety."

Christopher has the good graces to cringe, but does not back down. "We have unfinished business."

"No, *we* don't. I said everything I needed to say last week. Oh, wait, I do have something new."

"You do?"

I feel slightly guilty at the glimmer of hope in his eyes. "Tell your wife I'm sorry she's married to you and that you're a lying pig."

"And…" Somehow, he looks like he's expecting more.

"No, that's it. Now, what did you want?" I smile meanly at him.

"You don't have to be such a bitch," he says, face hardening.

"I know I don't have to, I want to." I pause and repeat my question harshly. "What do you want?"

"I wanted to talk about us," he says, sounding helpless and hopeless.

"There is no us."

"I love you. And, without putting words in your mouth, I think you love me too."

His confession momentarily stuns me and I soften my response. "We were casual from the beginning."

"Maybe *in* the beginning… didn't you feel something change?"

Did I? We had a lot of fun and I certainly enjoyed spending time with him. But, love? Maybe I sound shallow, but, no, I don't think it was ever love.

"No, Christopher, it was never love." I can't help it. I'm feeling sorry for him. "At least not on my end."

"You're lying to yourself."

"No. I'm not. Have you stopped to think that maybe you're the one lying to yourself?"

"Why would I do that? I knew the moment I met you that you were somebody special."

"You were married, *not* in an open relationship, and you cheated. You should look at that. This isn't about me at all."

"Of course it is," Christopher insists, sounding irritated. He steps forward and I involuntarily take a step backward. "Now you back away from me?" He sounds hurt and angry.

"I think I know why you've been lying to yourself."

Christopher looks surprised. "What?"

"I think that you think you're in love with me."

"I *am* in love with you."

"No," I correct him. "You're in love with the idea of me."

"What does that even mean?"

"I'm something new and exciting, without the instability of being with a drug addict."

"That's ridiculous." Christopher's eyes flash angrily.

"It's just a theory."

"You know what I think?"

"By all means, enlighten me."

"I think you're a slut who jumps into bed with anybody who will have her."

I feel like I've been slapped in the face. My blood is boiling. "A second ago, you said you loved me. Now I'm a slut? You and your crazy wife deserve each other."

"You're right."

"What?" Now, it's my turn to be surprised.

"I was in love with an idea. I thought you were a genuine free spirit who wanted me to be happy."

"Why would my goal be to make you happy?" I shake my head, as if clearing away the cobwebs. "Never mind. I think you should leave."

"You have all this self-righteous indignation, but you're not a dumb woman. You gave me the solution of an open marriage so you wouldn't have to feel any guilt over sleeping with a married man."

"You have that exactly backward. You used it as a way to dupe me into your bed. Leave. Now." My voice has risen slightly and his raises to match.

"Fine." He pauses. "I want my stuff back."

"Are you joking? I'm keeping the DVDs, CDs, whatever you gave me."

"Some of those were loans." I stare at him, aghast. He's completely serious. How did I ever think he was sane? My eye catches an object on my coffee table and I can't help myself.

"Too bad," I start. "I'm keeping the book you gave me." I stare at him resolutely. Two can play this childish game.

"Fine. Consider it payment for services rendered," he retorts.

"Oh, please. If I required payment, you couldn't begin to afford someone like me." My voice has returned to a conversational tone. "Now get out before I call the police and report an intruder."

Without another word, Christopher storms from the apartment, slamming the door for good measure. I barely make it to the couch before I collapse. I'm shaking. I didn't realize how much his odd behavior scared me. Maybe his wife isn't the only meth-head.

The door opens again and I immediately tense, wondering if Christopher is returning. Tension turns to relief just as fast.

"Are you okay? I could hear yelling and Christopher nearly ran me down trying to leave." Jane's barrage of words flows effortlessly as she comes to my side.

"I'm fine. It was just…spooky. I've never seen anybody get that angry and irrational."

"Are you sure you're okay?"

"Honest, I'm fine. I'm just shaken up. A stiff drink would do wonders." I laugh shakily.

"What happened? What was he even doing here?"

"I think it was meant to be some kind of reconciliation attempt."

"Oh, sure. All my attempts to win back exes involve threatening them in their homes."

"It started out that way, but it changed," I clarify with a lop-sided smile.

"What changed?"

"When I didn't immediately jump back into his arms, he didn't like it."

"Tough shit. That's no excuse." I could hear the anger in Jane's voice. I must look worse than I imagined.

"Relax. He's gone now and I doubt we'll ever hear from him again."

"Never would be too soon," Jane declares and we both laugh. "Now, about that drink."

CHAPTER FOUR

"What a crazy day on set," I announce, as I enter my apartment. Jane, seated at the kitchen table, looks upset. "What? What's the matter?"

"You got some messages."

"Messages? Nobody calls me on the landline."

"Today she did."

I pause in my approach to the answering machine at the use of the feminine pronoun. My heart sinking, I walk to the machine, note that it reveals I have twenty messages, and hit Play.

"I don't know who you think you are, talking to me like that. And in front of Christopher. You're not so special. You're not even that pretty." Click.

"I love him so much. You just don't understand. We were working out our problems before *you* came along. Why couldn't you find someone else to fuck?" Click.

"Bitch, bitch, bitch. I'd like to rip your fucking head off and set it on fire, you fucking cunt." Click. I press Stop and turn to face Jane, eyes wide.

"Are they all like that?"

"Worse. They get progressively weirder and more threatening."

"More threatening than wanting to rip my head off and set it on fire?"

"Oh yeah. The wife is crazy creative, emphasis on crazy."

I turn back to the machine and listen to the remaining seventeen messages. The last one actually consists of pulsing music, then silence, and finally one word whispered with as much malice as I've ever heard in one word.

"*Die.*"

"What are you going to do, Gracie?"

"I'm calling in the experts."

"You're calling the cops?"

"Hell, yeah," I tell Jane as I search online for the local, non-emergency police phone number.

"Will they do anything?"

"I don't know, but those are some pretty specific threats. I'm not taking any chances. I'm not going to be the idiot in the horror movie who does something stupid simply to advance the plot and ends up chopped into bits before the end credits role. I want to be in the sequel."

I've found the number and am dialing it on my cell phone when Jane asks, "We're in a horror movie?"

I stop dialing and close the phone.

"What are you doing? I thought you were calling the cops."

"I was, but you're right."

"Usually, but about what specifically this time?"

"What *are* they going to do? Sure the phone calls are creepy and even threatening. But, she hasn't done anything," I explain. I haven't set my phone down yet, I notice. Ambivalence?

"I thought you didn't want to be the girl in the movie who gets chopped into bits."

"That's still true."

"You can't be in the sequel if you're dead," Jane points out.

"That's also true." There's no denying that logic. "Maybe this will be the end of it," I suggest.

Jane actually snorts. "I thought she was a pissed-off meth head."

"Exactly."

"What do you mean, exactly?"

"In a week, she'll be focused on scoring more drugs. I'll be forgotten. She probably just needed to vent." At this point, I wonder if I'm trying to convince Jane or myself.

"Maybe," Jane agrees uneasily. She definitely doesn't sound convinced.

"Let's just wait and see what happens."

"Hey, it's your life. Just so we're clear, though. If she shows up here, I'm stepping aside and pointing to your bedroom door."

"Nice to know you've got my back," I reply dryly.

"Always."

CHAPTER FIVE

It's only been a week since that last awful fight with Christopher (and those crazy messages) and I still feel jittery. Honestly, I am having trouble figuring out why I've been so…traumatized. It's not like he hit me or anything. He just yelled. And, I yelled back. I've had this feeling all day like someone is watching me. I've even wheeled around suddenly to try and catch the person. Of course, there's never anybody there because nobody is following me.

I enter my apartment building and the feeling vanishes the instant the door closes. I take the stairs to my apartment. By the time I let myself in and sit down at my computer to check email, I've completely forgotten that sense of being watched. When someone knocks on my door ten minutes or so later, I bound over to the door with no hesitation.

"Coming," I sing out. I open the door and my smile fades in an instant. I try to close my door, but her arm shoots out and she barrels her way into my apartment, into my home.

"Come on in, Alicia," I mutter. As I close the door behind her, I momentarily consider running out of here. But, I don't want to leave her alone in my apartment. Who knows what she would do? It has yet to occur to me that she could do more than property damage.

I stand with my hands clutching the doorknob behind me, almost like a talisman. Alicia stands next to the couch staring at me.

"You look terrible," I speak without thinking and anger flares in her eyes.

"You would too, if your husband won't shut the fuck up." She stops, although it feels like a half-formed thought. I say nothing and she continues. "Don't you want to know what he won't shut up about?"

"I assume you're going to tell me?"

"Smart ass. One of these days, you're going to say something when you shouldn't and it'll be your last."

"Unless today is that day, why don't you leave?" Another person might interpret a surge of adrenaline as anxiety and thus watch her step; I apparently am merely emboldened by it.

"I'll leave when I'm finished," Alicia practically snarls at me.

"Are you high now?"

Alicia responds by taking a few angry steps in my direction. When I lose my smirk and cower slightly, she smiles. "Worried?"

I force myself to release the door handle and walk nonchalantly toward her, stopping about three feet away. Miraculously, my voice sounds steady in my ears as I ask, "What do you want, Alicia?"

"Do you think all Christopher talks about is you?"

"I hope not."

"Well, he doesn't."

"That's good, right?"

"He keeps talking about us, our relationship." For some reason, inexplicable to me, this seems to make her angry.

"Isn't that what most wives want?"

"Not if the husband is trying to remake the relationship." If looks could kill, I'd be dead, and I'm still confused.

"If there are problems, doesn't it make sense to make changes?" I ask the question as delicately as I can, sensing I can never be delicate enough.

"Not if the model for the wife role is his whore of a mistress," Alicia hisses at me. I take a step back. A wave of fear moves through me.

"Look, I am sorry about all of this," I hurry to say before she can continue. "I've already told you that Christopher said he had an open marriage."

"He lied."

"I know that now," I say in exasperation, "but I didn't know that then. I don't understand why you're still mad at me. I'm not in love with him – it was only a casual relationship. He's the one you should be talking to."

"You poor thing," Alicia says, her voice dripping with pity.

"I'm sorry?" The sudden change in content and tone of the conversation startles me. The calm before the rest of the friggin' hurricane, perhaps?

"You're deluding yourself."

"How so?" I'm genuinely curious.

"You're either so insecure about relationships that you deliberately choose ones with no future," she begins.

"I can't wait to hear my second choice," I interrupt sarcastically.

"Or," Alicia stresses, "you fell in love with my husband and are attempting to reduce it to a mere fling to spare yourself a tragic emotional wound."

Pretty good for a meth-head, I think, but wisely, for once, don't say. I remain silent.

"Either way, you're pathetic."

I tense as she walks past me, but she simply goes to the door.

Opening it, she turns back to deliver a parting shot before leaving.

"If you come near my husband again, I'll kill you." She smiles viciously and is gone.

"Holy shit," I exclaim to the empty room. All of the adrenaline that has been coursing through my veins during our chat suddenly overwhelms me. I feel like I am going to jump out of my skin but instead begin talking to myself as I pace around my living room.

"She thinks I'm pathetic? She feels sorry for me? Oh, please. I'm not the one married to a man who not only sleeps with other women, he formed an emotional attachment to at least one." I sit down on the couch with a loud exhalation.

"If I wanted him, I could have him. But, I'm the delusional one? She can have the poor, confused man. I'm extricating myself from this mess." I'm feeling calmer and I actually laugh. "I was just in it for the sex." Even if that's not true, saying it makes me calmer.

So, boys and girls, what did we learn from all of this? Married men are off-limits.

CHAPTER SIX

I'm so nervous I can barely stay seated in the metal folding chair on which I perch. The room is closet-small, as a waiting room should be, I suppose, and relatively bare. There are a half-dozen metal folding chairs and nothing else. I'd worry about the legitimacy of this production if I weren't so keenly aware of the high cost of rent in this city. I clutch my audition sides tightly in one hand, alternately running lines in my head and informing myself that I suck. Did I mention that one of the benefits of sticking to no line or bit parts is that there's never any anxiety?

I mentally slap myself and tell myself to focus, that the director asked for me personally, and that I worked hard to prepare for this audition. I take a deep breath and do, in fact, feel more relaxed. There are only four other women apparently scheduled for this time slot, all physically different from each other and from me. Apparently, the casting director isn't interested in a specific type. Except for young and attractive, of course.

"Ms. Corsini?" The slightly built man who greeted me when I arrived interrupts my reverie with his question.

"Yes?"

"You can go in now." He offers me a toothy smile that I automatically return. "Break a leg."

"Thanks."

Amazingly, as I enter the room, I feel all of my anxiety about the audition melt away. I've prepared for this and I'm ready. I glance around the room, getting my bearings. It's larger than the waiting room, though not by much, and there are three men and a camera. An older man in glasses, wearing khakis and a button-down shirt (with the top two buttons undone, of course) addresses me first.

"I'm Benjamin Eckley, the director."

"I'm Roger Short, the casting director," says the scrawny, probably thirty-something, man in the middle. He's wearing jeans and a Ramones concert shirt. His Converse-clad feet seem to tap to a beat only he can hear. I remember that he's the one who called Catherine about me as he continues talking. "I saw you in a two-minute scene playing the teacher of the abused boy in *Stopping the Pain*. I thought you were beautiful and riveting."

"Thank you very much," I manage to say. It was barely a scene. I can't believe I was that memorable.

"I've been waiting for a larger part to better showcase your talent."

"I'm glad to be here auditioning."

Roger turns to the third guy, indicating that he should introduce himself.

"I'm Sam Starling, the DP." Although the name didn't sound it, this guy looks like an Irish stereotype with red hair, freckles, and blue eyes. He has fine lines around his eyes, but otherwise his face seems young, almost babyish.

The director, casting director, and director of photography are all here, is what I'm thinking as Benjamin goes through the standard audition spiel.

"Roger will read Damian, the male character's lines, so look at him and not in the camera, after you slate." I nod and he tells me to begin.

"Hello, I'm Graciella Corsini. My agent is Catherine Rodham. Her number is 917-555-2942." I take a breath and shift my gaze to Roger. I produce the dialogue effortlessly, the words falling from my lips as though I was Becky, the character for whom I am auditioning. Apparently, the guys agree.

"That was perfect," Benjamin states. "Normally, I like to give notes after a first read and make adjustments, but I don't know what I would say. That's exactly how I hear her in my head."

"You did a wonderful job," Roger agrees.

"What is your availability?" Benjamin asks.

"I'm available whenever you need me," I immediately answer.

"Great," Benjamin says. "We still have a handful of actresses to audition. Normally we'd do callbacks, to see chemistry with the actor cast as Damian. He's wrapping a project in Vegas, though, so we can't. We'll be casting without. We should have a final decision within a week at the latest."

"That sounds great," I say and smile. "I look forward to hearing from you when you make the decision." And then it's over.

CHAPTER SEVEN

"What's the matter?" I ask Jane this question before I can tell her how fabulously well the audition went. She is standing next to the couch and gestures toward the coffee table.

"These arrived for you."

"What? Someone sent me flowers?" There's something wrong with the flowers, so I walk closer. "They're black," I stupidly state the obvious.

"Yep."

"They're not dead, though." I peer at a few petals. "Are they spray-painted?"

"Yep."

"Someone sent me flowers spray-painted black."

"Yep."

The monosyllabic answers are tiresome, so I ask a question that can't be answered yes or no. "Who delivered them?"

"They weren't delivered," Jane sighs and sits on the couch.

"How'd they get here?"

"They were left on our doorstep."

"Why'd you bring them in?"

"I wasn't about to leave creepy black flowers on the doorstep for the entire floor to see."

"You could have thrown them away."

"No, I thought I'd leave them for you."

"Right." A question occurs to me. "How do you know they aren't for you?" Jane gives me an incredulous look. "Was there a card?"

"As a matter of fact," Jane begins, to my surprise, "there was." She holds out a tiny white florist's envelope. I take it and join her on the couch.

" 'For that bitch, Gracie'," I read aloud. "Guess they are for me." I sigh dramatically. "Let me give you some advice, Jane."

"What?"

"Don't ever date the husband of a meth-head."

Jane laughs. "Shouldn't be a problem."

"Hey, you never know," I say with a tone of warning. "If you had told me a few months ago that this would have happened, I would have laughed too. Now I get threatening phone calls and black roses."

"She's charming," Jane snorts. "No wonder her husband strayed."

"Besides. I'm irresistible."

"Modest, too." Jane becomes serious again. "Do you think we should do something?"

"Like what? I still think she's run out of steam and this will end."

"I hope you're right – though you said the same thing after the phone messages. Just remember your horror movie analogy."

"I know, I know. I remember. I promise I'm not gonna end up chopped into little pieces because I ignored all the warning signs of the psycho and didn't call the police," I assure her.

"If you think so."

"I do." Don't I? A little voice inside wonders if I'm underestimating the depth of Alicia's rage. I choose to ignore that voice. I realize that I've overlooked something.

"Hey, I'm sorry that this is impacting you, too," I say to Jane. She appears surprised by the apology. "What?"

"You weren't involved in my indiscretion, but because you live with me, I could be putting you in danger." Just saying those words aloud makes the situation feel all the more real and dire.

"Hey," Jane says softly, "this isn't your fault. You don't have to apologize. And while I certainly appreciate your concern for my well-being, I wish you had more concern for your own."

"Toss the flowers in the garbage. Let me tell you about my fabulous audition," I deftly change the subject.

CHAPTER EIGHT

I finally capitulated to my mother's demands for a family dinner and am on my way to Brooklyn. It's Saturday evening and I enjoy people-watching on the subway as I travel to my parents' brownstone. I'm running late, which is never a good thing when it comes to my mother, and I can hear the noise from the packed house even before I open the door to let myself in.

"Hey, everybody," I sing out. "Sorry I'm late." My mother, Annabella, is in the kitchen, putting the finishing touches on the lasagna, and heavenly smells waft from the room. My mother stands about 5 feet tall and has just in the past few years begun thickening in the middle. You can't eat spaghetti and gelato forever without eventually paying the price. She has beautiful brown eyes and curly brown hair like mine, although she almost always has it pulled back in a bun. She rarely cuts it, but she complains that it gets in her eyes when she's cooking or sewing. She works as a neighborhood seamstress because she loves working with her hands.

"Why can't you ever be on time, Graciella?" Oh yeah, my mother absolutely refuses to call me Gracie like everybody else.

My given name is Graciella and, by God, that's what she intends to call me.

"What would you have to complain about if I were on time, Mama?" I tease her good-naturedly as I cross to her side and give her a quick hug. She chuckles softly and I take the two steps to the kitchen table.

My brother and sister are seated at the table with my father, and everybody has a glass of wine. I pour myself a glass and join them. My sister and my father are arguing about, what else, college. My little sister is 18 years old and a sophomore at New York University. She got some strange genes from somewhere in the family and is 5'10" tall, about 110 pounds, with beautiful olive skin and straight raven black hair. Over the past year, she has been modeling on a fairly regular basis and wants to drop out of college. You've heard the expression, over my dead body? Yeah, that about sums up my father's views on the subject.

My father, Tomas, is your stereotypical Italian father. He came over from the Old Country in his teens with nothing but the shirt on his back and has worked his way up, doing…something for the city. What? I couldn't tell you. Believe it or not, he's shorter than I am, stocky, and although approaching 60 years old, has a shockingly full head of dark brown hair.

"How many times must we talk about this, Maria?"

"As many times until you can understand that this is what I want."

"You are in one of the top schools in the country – on a scholarship – and you want to throw it all away."

"But, it's my life. Besides, Gracie doesn't even use her degree."

"Hey, now, don't drag me into your argument," I protest.

"Well, it's true. What does an English degree have to do with acting?"

"Absolutely nothing." Sometimes agreeing is the easiest way to be dismissed from a disagreement.

"See," Maria defiantly states to our father. "Gracie's degree has nothing to do with her career."

"She finished school and so will you," my father says, completely ignoring my sister's attempt to make a point.

And so it goes, but I tune them out. I sip at my glass of Chianti and just enjoy the company of my family. Eventually, the conversation ends, as always, with no resolution. This likely suits my father just fine, because it means that Maria will remain in school while she continues to try and win him over. As much as she may threaten, she will never leave school without my parents' blessing and they will never give it.

"Earth to Gracie," my older brother whispers in my direction. I focus on his face. He's another one who got some unusual genes. He's only about 5'8" tall, but since he is a New York City fireman, he is in excellent shape. With his blond hair and blue eyes, though, he looks like he was adopted. He turned thirty this year and has begun talking about settling down, although he continues to play the field as far as I know.

"Yes, Anthony," I respond with a smile.

"What's new with you?"

"I landed a large supporting part in a new movie." This gets everybody's attention and I tell them all about the audition for Becky. "I begin filming next week," I finish and they are all suitably impressed.

"How's Jane doing?" My mother loves my roommate because she cooks for a living and mama is forever trying to get Jane to come with me to family dinners. Mama frequently says if I'm not going to bring a boy with me, I might as well bring Jane.

"Jane is doing well. She's been getting more dinner shifts and thinks they may be grooming her to take over as a primary chef.

I think there's a term for it, but I don't know," I explain Jane's career trajectory.

Dinner is ready and my brother assists my mother in setting the food out on the table. We continue to talk about everything and nothing, often quite loudly, as we dish ourselves some of the best Italian in the city. The noise level can be intimidating to outsiders, who think we're fighting with each other. In addition, if you want to actually have a chance to speak, once we're all at the table, you better be ready to interrupt. A couple of hours later and I am ready to return to the relative quiet of the street. Hugs all around and then I take my leave.

I marvel at the members of my family as I walk back to the subway station. We tease each other and give each other a hard time, but our love is strong… and lord help the individual who tries to mess with one of us. We're like the Mafia; we take care of our own.

CHAPTER NINE

"Welcome, Gracie. Thanks again for accepting the role of Becky," Benjamin Eckley, the director, greets me as I arrive on set.

My part as Becky, the girlfriend of the lead character, Damian, is the largest I've ever had. I'm guessing it'll probably amount to about twenty minutes of screen time. It's like starring in a short film. But, I digress.

"Hi, Ben, thanks for offering me the part. I'm excited to play such a pivotal role."

"Good, great. I assume you got the shooting schedule for the day," Ben says.

"Of course. I'm ready to go."

"Come with me, then." Ben leads me through the restaurant in which we'll be filming several scenes today. It looks like an authentic family-owned Italian restaurant. And, since we're in Little Italy, it probably is. Ben's comments to me as we walk through the kitchen prep area answer my unspoken questions.

"This restaurant is over fifty years old, established by the children of Italian immigrants. Now it's owned by one of the siblings' sons, the brother of a guy I went to school with back in the day. That's why they're letting us use the place for the restaurant scene, and also why we need to be done by 4 p.m. On Sundays, they only do dinner. On Mondays, they're closed, so we'll do most of the filming then."

"That's cool. It's a beautiful place. If the food is half as good as the décor, it'd be amazing." You might be thinking I'm laying on the flattery a little thick, but I'm honestly blown away. Instead of the stereotypical still life with fruit artwork and red-n-white checkerboard tablecloths, the walls are decorated with reproductions of the work of Italian masters and the tablecloths look like white linen. That's just for starters. We've arrived at our destination, however, so I'm forced to focus.

"We're still waiting for Adam. He's playing Damian. While we're waiting, Melissa will work with you. Okay? Okay." Ben is gone before I can respond. I turn to Melissa, a woman of somewhat indeterminate age, with her blond hair pulled back in a loose ponytail.

"I'm in your hands."

Melissa's brown eyes glint and she rubs her hands together in mock devilish glee while I laugh. She has a rack of clothing behind her and has arranged the chairs in what I can only imagine is a back office, facing each other in front of a large, but portable, mirror that I assume is hers.

"These are your outfits for the scenes today," Melissa indicates three outfits hanging together on the rack. "I trust the sizes you gave Ben were accurate. Normally, I like to have fittings, but I was wrapping another film."

"No worries. I promise I gave Ben my true sizes. Do you really do all this? Hair, makeup, and wardrobe?" I'm quite amazed.

"Yes, I do. I started out doing hair and makeup only before realizing I have an eye for clothing as well. I don't sew terribly well, though. I usually find stuff. Plus, I do have a seamstress if I need anything more complicated done than fixing a button or raising a hem."

"Nobody's perfect," I respond and Melissa laughs. We get down to business. When Ben knocks on the door, we're sitting across from each other, gabbing away as if we'd known each other all our lives.

"Ready?"

"Whenever you are." I'm already rising out of my seat.

"Come on out and let Adam get ready."

Adam enters the room, around Ben, hand outstretched. "Nice to finally meet you, Gracie."

"You, too, Adam." I'm pleased to note that Adam is attractive. After all, if you're going to pretend you're a couple, it seems it would be helpful to find each other attractive.

"Looks like it's my turn to get pretty. See you on set in a few."

I leave with Ben and we walk back into the dining area. Several table and chair sets have been pushed around to make room for multiple lights, as well as the cameras and equipment. One table and chair set is clearly intended for our first scene. Although my character's death triggers the primary plot of the movie, we have several scenes first, intended to establish our relationship.

When Adam is ready, we commence filming. But, let me jump ahead to the end of the day on my second day of filming when things really get interesting. In fact, it isn't even connected to filming. Or so I think at the time anyway.

Filming wraps after the second day and we say our good byes. Yesterday, Adam had walked with me to the subway station, but today is a different story.

"Are you ready to head out?" I ask after I gather up my belongings.

"Actually, I'm going to help Ben and Sam pack everything up before I go."

"Oh, do you want some more help? I wouldn't mind staying."

"That's okay, Gracie. We've got it covered," Adam insists.

"If you're sure," I respond uncertainly.

"It's fine. We'll see you next Sunday."

"The day of my untimely death," I sigh with mock sadness. Adam smiles.

"I'm already sad thinking about it."

"Yeah, I can tell," I retort.

Adam laughs. "See you next week, Gracie."

"See you. Bye, Ben, bye, Sam," I call out to them in the back.

"Bye, Gracie," I hear in stereo from the guys.

With a final wave to Adam, I leave the restaurant and begin walking toward the station. Not two blocks later, however, I pass the proverbial dark alley.

Now it's only early evening, so it's not pitch black, but with the sun setting behind buildings, there are lots of dark shadows. It certainly looks sinister enough to me. Especially when I become cognizant of the evident exchange between the alley's two equally shadowy occupants. Instead of continuing to walk on like a good oblivious New Yorker, I stop to watch.

The man on the left, a skinny guy, probably about my age, is wearing baggy pants and a Knicks shirt with a baseball cap on backwards. Do people still wear ball caps backwards?

Skinny Guy hands a wad of cash to a taller man of average build, also appearing to be in his twenties. Average Guy tucks the money away inside his jacket and extracts a baggy of white powder. Not a small bag, but not hefty either. Okay, so I guess it isn't that shadowy after all, at least not physically. But, those are certainly some nefarious goings-on. My curious mind is wondering what's in the bag (cocaine, heroin?) and who the guys are (supplier, mid-level distributor?) when both men simultaneously become aware of my presence in the street and turn in my direction. Skinny Guy palms the bag and immediately takes off in the opposite direction. Average Guy puts on a fake solicitous smile and begins walking toward me.

Toward me? Logic dictates that I run. Somehow my brain is unable to send the signal to my feet. Adrenaline coursing through me that is supposed to signal fight or flight surely cannot be expecting me to fight. Flight, damn it, that's the correct response.

"Can I help you, miss?" Average Guy stops about five feet from my position and asks this question in a voice of solicitude as fake as his smile. I mirror the smile and hope my voice doesn't squeak when I speak.

"Not at all. I didn't even see you there. I do that sometimes." That's a good lie. Go with that.

"What?"

"What? Oh, stop randomly on the sidewalk when I'm lost in thought." I'm now thinking this sounds lame, but Average Guy only nods.

"Of course. I'll be on my way, then." And, he is. He walks away from me, in the direction of the restaurant.

"Thank you for asking," I call after him, then resolutely continue walking toward the subway station. It takes everything in me not to turn around to check if he's watching. I don't breathe again until the subway doors close and he is *not* on the train with me.

*****

"Are you insane?"

I've finished telling Jane my story and this is her response. "Thanks, that's helpful," I reply drolly.

"I'm not trying to be helpful. You could have been killed." She seems genuinely quite frightened on my behalf. I, on the other hand, having made it out alive, am now acting as though it meant absolutely nothing. False bravado? Maybe.

"By a low-level drug dealer? I doubt it," I say with utter confidence.

"A low-level? Do you hear yourself?" Jane sounds exasperated, a tone frequently employed by people in conversation with me.

"What?" Her reaction genuinely perplexes me. "I'm okay. I got out of there alive."

"This time." Jane bites at her lower lip, confirming her anxiety.

"There's not going to be a next time," I try to soothe her.

"You don't know that."

"It's not like I run around looking for people in the act of committing crimes."

"You just need to be more careful."

"That's enough, Jane. My story would never upset you this much. What's really going on?"

Jane looks near tears. "Nothing."

I'm becoming alarmed. "Don't tell me, nothing. You're about to burst into tears. What happened?"

"Nothing," she insists as she stares at her feet, unable to meet my gaze.

"Did something happen? Is everyone we know okay? You're starting to freak me out here."

Jane rises from the couch and walks toward the door. "Come with me." I do. She leads me down the stairs to the building's garbage cans. As usual, they're filled to capacity. She reaches for a shoebox sitting on top of the pile of refuse. I get a sick feeling in the pit of my stomach.

"I didn't want to show you this. Since you insisted." Jane's eyes are red when she looks at me. "I can't open it again." I take the box from her.

With one deep, shuddering breath, I steel myself for what I may be about to see. I open the top with one quick motion and stare in abject horror at the contents. The box is filled with blood and hair.

"Is that a guinea pig?" I can barely whisper the question.

"Yes," comes the reply. Jane faces away from me.

"It's been… cut into pieces." My stomach has begun roiling in emotional protest.

"Yes," Jane says again.

I close the lid, place the box back in a can, and immediately begin dry heaving. Thank goodness I hadn't eaten in hours. My mind is reeling. "Where did that come from?"

"It was on our doorstep when I got home from work this afternoon."

"Someone sent it?"

"Apparently."

"Who would, who could…do something like *that*?" Like a thief in the night, a name sneaks into my head. By the look on Jane's face, the name has already occurred to her. "Even Alicia would never do something like this," I protest, though my protestation sounds weak to my own ears.

"Who else could it be?"

I can honestly, thankfully, think of nobody we know. "Why? Why would she do that? I don't care how angry she is at me, this is horrible."

"Haven't you seen *Fatal Attraction*?"

I shoot her a look. "Let's go back upstairs," I say, without answering the question.

Back in the apartment, sitting on the couch, a question arises. "Do you think she's calling me a pig?"

"What?" Jane sounds confused at my question.

"The animal in the box was a guinea pig. Do you think she meant it as a message?"

"Calling you a pig?"

"Calling me a pig."

"Doesn't that level of subtlety seem out of reach for a meth addict?"

"Maybe. I don't know. I don't want to think about it, anymore," I whine in frustration.

"At what point will you pull your head out of the sand?"

"What? What are you talking about?"

"Alicia left you a series of threatening messages. She sent you roses painted black. She verbally assaulted you in our home. Now she's killed and mutilated an animal. At what point do you admit she's out of control and you might be in danger?"

"You weren't even going to tell me about the guinea pig. How can you be angry at my reaction?"

"Well, now you know."

"We don't know Alicia did this."

"You're kidding, right?"

I sigh. "You're right. Let me call Christopher and ask him to speak with her. If it doesn't stop, I'll call the police. How does that sound?"

"You'll call the police if she does one more thing, no matter how small?"

"Yes, I promise."

"Good."

"Jane?"

"What?" She sounds peevish.

"I'm so sorry it hasn't stopped."

"I know you are," Jane says, sounding less peevish.

"I'll fix it. I promise."

"I know you will, Gracie."

*****

That was the end of that until I met with Christopher later in the week.

"Thank you for meeting me, Christopher."

"Of course. You sounded so upset on the phone."

"After the way things ended, I wasn't sure you'd come. This isn't something to discuss over the phone."

"What is it? What's going on?" I hear the worry in his voice and I'm glad; I hope it means he'll listen with an open mind.

"It started several weeks ago."

"Around the time of our fight."

"Um, yes. Things started happening." I know I am dancing around the issue. How do you tell a man his crazy wife seems to be stalking you?

"What things?"

"First, it was a dozen threatening messages in one day."

"Threatening, how?"

"They started vague and then were…pretty clear." I hear the hesitation in my voice.

"What did they say, exactly?" Christopher tries to sound matter-of-fact with his question.

"Just threats. Anyway," I hurry on, "a week or so later, roses spray-painted black arrived."

"Who sent them?" Christopher is past worried and clearly alarmed.

"There wasn't a name on the card," I sidestep the question. "Then, earlier this week, a new package arrived." I pause and Christopher simply waits for me to finish. "There was a dead guinea pig in it." Christopher's face goes white. "It had been…sliced apart." When I finish, my voice is barely a whisper and Christopher is even whiter.

"Who?"

"You know who."

"She couldn't." He offers protestation as weakly as I did with Jane earlier, perfunctorily, as if knowing he should defend his wife's honor.

"She did," I say flatly. "This was after she came to my home and yelled at me."

"She went to your apartment?"

"Yes. I want it to stop."

"Of course." He seems dazed.

"Listen to me." Our eyes meet. "So far, I haven't gone to the police. My roommate has laid down the law, however. One more thing, and I mean the barest incident, and I *will* call the police."

"I understand."

"Do you?" Part of me hates how harsh my tone has gotten, but the bigger part knows he needs to really hear me.

"Yes, yes, I do," Christopher insists. "I swear to God that this will stop. I can't believe she would." I must have quite a look on my face because he stops mid-sentence. "Never mind. I am so sorry."

"Thank you." Suddenly, fatigue threatens to overwhelm me. Apprehension over telling a man about his psycho wife is apparently physically draining. I smile tiredly and Christopher smiles back, the relief evident.

"I will take care of it tonight. I promise."

"I know that you'll try," I correct him. "And you know the consequences if you fail." His smile falters slightly. He stands to leave.

"Be well," is all he says and is gone.

I unlock my phone to call Jane.

"Well, that was awkward," I say with no introduction or preamble.

"Is it done?"

"It's done."

"Good. See you at home?"

"See you soon." I snap the phone shut. I drink my espresso and wait for the caffeine rush. Not that I need it.

CHAPTER TEN

Life is wonderful. Christopher must have spoken to his wife by now and yet there's been no crazy retaliatory action in the days since. The sun is shining and it's a beautiful day. I wrap filming on my first semi-major film role on Sunday. And, more importantly, I am on my way to an audition for a recurring role on *Heart's Home*. I bombed three auditions in the past week, maybe due to nervousness about the whole Christopher and Alicia debacle. I don't know. Either way, I'm ready for a reversal of fortune.

Catherine called me this morning to see if I was free. Free? To audition for the hottest daytime soap ever? Like she even had to ask? Even better, for the initial audition, the casting director is letting me use a prepared monologue rather than do a cold reading. According to Catherine, she has a son with dyslexia and was sympathetic to my plight. Yes, I finally told Catherine my dyslexia issue.

As I step through the doors into the studio building, the butterflies in my stomach settle and I'm ready to roll. I breeze through security and head for the reception desk.

"Hello. Graciella Corsini, here to see Meg Ashton."

"Go through the double doors behind me, turn to the right. It's the second office on the left."

I thank her and walk to the office. This is obviously not a cattle call kind of situation. There's no way she'd audition more than a few women in her private office. I arrive and knock on the partially open door.

"Yes?"

"Ms. Ashton?"

"Yes. What can I do for you?"

You can cast me is on the tip of my tongue, but I only identify myself as I slightly push the door open further.

"Oh, hi. Come in, come in," I hear the casting director's voice, as well as the sound of her chair moving. The door suddenly opens wide and Meg Ashton stands before me. I am momentarily stunned. Normally you don't think of what a behind-the-scenes person looks like, but she is gorgeous. She's wearing a muted red jacket over jeans, the color perfectly complementing her shiny, jet black hair, and caramel coloring. The shape of her eyes has me suspecting both black and Asian ancestry.

"Please, call me Meg," she insists, walking back to her desk and indicating a plush chair in which I should sit.

"Thank you for seeing me, Meg," I start, "and for allowing me to use a monologue."

"No problem," Meg replies, waving her recently manicured nails at me. "My nine-year-old is also dyslexic, so I know how hard it can be to read unfamiliar material."

"I appreciate it."

She smiles, revealing perfectly white and straight teeth, and I smile in return.

"You're welcome, Gracie. Are you ready?"

"Absolutely."

"Great. I'd like you to do your monologue to me as if we're having a conversation. I don't want it to feel like acting, or staged in anyway. Okay?"

I nod and she signals to begin. I recite that monologue exactly as if we're having a conversation. I nail it beautifully. I can feel it and I can read it on Meg's face when I finish.

"That was fabulous."

"Thanks."

"As I'm sure you're aware, normally the casting director acts enigmatic about the audition. Maybe you get a call later for a callback or to be offered a part. Maybe you don't." She pauses expectantly.

"Yeah, that's usually how it goes," I say, not sure what response she wants.

"I'm holding the actual audition tomorrow morning and normally I would wait to see those women before inviting anyone to callbacks. I have a good feeling about you, though."

I'm biting the inside flesh of my cheek in order to contain my excitement.

"I'd like to officially invite you to the callbacks next Tuesday morning at 9 – you can schedule with the receptionist on your way out."

"Thank you so much," I say, gushing just a tiny bit. "This is a great opportunity."

"Here are the sides for the audition. I trust you can have this memorized by next week?" Meg hands me three pages of partial scenes, along with a character description.

"Absolutely. As long as I have several days, and my roommate is available to help, I can actually memorize a fair amount of material at a time."

"Then I'll see you back here on Tuesday." Taking that as my cue to leave, I stand and offer my hand.

"It was a pleasure to meet you. I'll see you Tuesday."

She smiles and nods as we shake hands goodbye. I exit, closing the door softly behind me.

After confirming with the receptionist, I head for home, my brain swirling with thoughts. I open my cell phone and text message Catherine the information about callbacks on Tuesday and then I call Jane. She answers on the first ring.

"So?"

"It went great!"

"Yay!"

"She invited me to callbacks before even holding the general audition."

"Fantastic! What do you have to prepare?"

"I've got three pages of dialogue. Can you help me?"

"Of course — as long as you don't forget me when you're famous."

"Never," I chuckle.

"When are the callbacks?"

"Next Tuesday morning."

"Good, that should give us plenty of time to make you perfect."

"I don't know about the perfect part," I reply with a laugh, "but it's definitely enough time to memorize the lines."

"If she liked you that much, she invited you early to return, I'm thinking maybe you have a leg up on the competition."

"That's nice to think, but I don't want to blow anything out of proportion. She hasn't even seen anybody else."

"That makes sense. We'll start working tomorrow?"

"Sounds great, Jane. See you at home later."

"See ya."

We end the call as I reach the subway station. I don't know for sure, but I think I had a big old smile on my face all the way home. *That part is mine* was the refrain in my head. *That part is mine.*

CHAPTER ELEVEN

I arrive in Little Italy earlier than the cast call time for my final day of filming the feature film, but of course, the crew has already arrived. I say my hellos as I walk through the restaurant back toward my makeshift dressing room.

"Are you ready for your death scene?" is how Melissa greets me when I enter the room. I put my hands to my throat in the universal sign of choking and pretend to roll my eyes into the back of my head. "Nice," she comments with a laugh.

"I'm excited because I've never died on camera before," I tell her. "I've always wanted to be a dead body on one of those forensic shows."

"That's creepy."

"Yeah, weird, I know." I giggle. "I just think it would be a blast."

"You're a strange girl, Gracie."

"So I've been told."

Melissa gets down to business. "In the scenes today, Damian proposes to Becky and shortly thereafter, while he's in the bathroom, the bad guy comes in and kills everyone in the place.

Damian comes out, sees you dead on the floor and then your part is concluded. Correct?"

"Correct."

"I have a lovely cocktail dress for you to wear. And we'll do slightly more exotic makeup, with upswept hair, leaving a few loose tendrils around your face."

"I'll be the most beautiful dead fiancée," I comment.

Hearing noise from out front, we both turn toward the open door. Seconds later, Adam pops his head in to greet us.

"Hello, ladies."

"Hey, Adam. How's it going?"

"Pretty well, Gracie. I filmed a new commercial this week. Nice payout."

"Congrats. Commercials are great that way."

"No doubt. Hey, Melissa. What's your plan for me today?"

"Hi, Adam." Melissa has gotten up and is removing a subtle pinstriped suit from the clothes rack. "Go get changed into this while I do Gracie's hair and makeup. Then we'll switch." She checks her watch. "I know Benjamin is hoping to begin in about thirty minutes." Adam takes his suit and disappears.

While Melissa does my hair, I tell her about the drug deal I saw after filming the prior week.

"You did not see that," she exclaims, astounded.

"It was totally surreal."

"He looked right at you?"

"He spoke to me!"

"Weren't you scared?"

"More afterward. I think I was too in shock at what I was seeing in the moment."

"I think I would have peed on myself."

I laugh. "I guess you don't know what you'll do until you're in the situation."

"I suppose. There," Melissa declares. "Your hair is finished."

I am quiet while she applies my makeup.

"Are you ready for me yet?" Adam stands in the doorway, while Melissa eyes her handiwork.

"Just give me," she applies some final powder, "one second. Finished. Off you go." I hop out of the chair, grab my dress, and head to the bathroom to change.

I stand in front of the mirror, marveling as always about what a talented artist can do. I look, not just hot, but smokin' hot. The dress is sleeveless, fastening around my neck in a halter style. It is fitted and drapes asymmetrically to above my knees. The deep emerald color goes beautifully with my coloring.

"I would want to look like this when someone proposes," I tell my reflection with a smile. I exit the bathroom and hang out on set with the crew until Adam is ready.

"Oh boy, don't you two make a picture," the director of photography comments when Adam appears.

"Thanks, man," Adam replies.

"That comment included you, too, beautiful," Sam says to me.

"Thank you very much, of course," I reply.

Sam's right. Adam and I look great together. We take our seats at the table and chat softly while the lighting is set.

"Damian would be a fool not to propose to someone who looks like that in a dress."

"Becky would be a fool not to say yes."

"Melissa mentioned you saw a drug deal just a couple of blocks from here and the guy talked to you."

"Yeah. Strange, right?"

"Maybe he was trying to decide whether or not he could trust you."

"Trust me?"

"You know, to keep your mouth shut."

I laugh. "You've seen too many movies."

"I guess so," Adam agrees, chuckling with me.

The director is ready, so Adam and I quit talking and focus on the scene. It takes a couple of hours to get all of the angles and distances for the proposal scene, but we finish in time for lunch.

Adam, Melissa, and I are eating fabulous Italian, courtesy of the restaurant owner, when I nearly choke on the bite I just took.

"Are you okay?" Adam and the others look uncertain as I cough.

"I'm fine," I manage to say. They look relieved and in a few moments I'm completely recovered. At least from the near choking. My head is still reeling from what I just saw.

"Did any of you see the man who came in the front?" All heads swivel to the empty front of the restaurant.

"What man?" Melissa asks.

"The man Ben walked back outside with moments ago."

They respond in the negative.

"You're never going to believe this." I still couldn't quite believe what I had just seen myself.

"What?" Melissa is about to fall out of her seat.

"I swear that the man Ben just walked outside with was the drug dealer I saw the other night."

"No way," Adam immediately says.

"Are you sure?" Melissa looks unsure as she asks this question.

"I am positive that the man is the drug dealer I saw last week."

"What are you going to do?" Melissa asks.

"I don't know. What can I do?" Our heads swivel toward the front door when we hear it open.

"I think you're about to get a chance to do something," Adam says, his voice barely above a whisper. We watch Ben and the stranger walk toward us. The closer they get, the more certain I am that the stranger is the drug dealer. My certainty is all but confirmed as I see a subtle change on the stranger's face when he recognizes me. My furtive glance to Melissa tells me she saw the recognition too.

"This is Tommy Pullman," Ben introduces Average Guy from the other night. "This is Melissa Fullerton, our artistic genius; Adam Gafferty, our lead actor, and Gracie Corsini, our pivotal supporting actress." Ben looks briefly around. "And Sam's probably out at the truck."

Everyone dutifully shakes hands with Tommy, who, unless it is in my fevered imagination, lingers over my hand and name.

"Gracie Corsini, it's nice to meet you," Tommy says formally.

"It's nice to meet you, too, Tommy Pullman," I respond the same, hoping I sound as nonchalant as I definitely do not feel.

"That's a beautiful name for a beautiful lady," Tommy continues.

"Thank you very much," I say, with an almost genuine smile. Compliments are compliments – even when coming from drug dealers. Adam arches an eyebrow at the saccharine flattery.

"Tommy is an associate of one of the major financial backers of this film."

If I had been drinking when Ben made this comment, it would have come out my nose. As it is, I make a small, strangled noise in my throat. Nobody reacts.

"Yes, my boss is interested in supporting the arts. He asked me to check on his investment. When I was here last week, Ben invited me to come back when more of the cast and crew would be present."

"Who is your boss?" I try to look as innocent as I can while asking this question.

Tommy looks blandly at me. "EKG Enterprises. It's a boring investment firm."

"Oh," is all I can think to say. Thankfully, Sam's return saves me from more inanity. His noise breaks the silence.

"We'd better get back to filming. We've only got a couple of hours left," Ben explains to Tommy as he walks the drug dealer/financial backer to the front door. Their conversation becomes inaudible.

"I can't believe you asked him who his boss is," Melissa says as soon as the men are out of earshot.

"That was pretty ballsy," Adam agrees.

"Do you think so?" A note of uncertainty enters into my voice. "I wasn't trying to get myself in trouble." I sigh. "I'm too nosy for my own good."

"I wouldn't worry about it," Melissa offers, trying to assuage my sudden fears.

"I'm sure he won't be waiting for you when we finish filming today," Adam teases.

"Thanks, that's helpful," I say, my voice dripping with sarcasm.

Ben returns at that moment. "Everybody ready. It's time for Becky to die." Ben laughs and heads for his camera. Although he's (obviously) speaking of the character, I exchange uneasy glances with Melissa and Adam before following Ben.

Despite my gesture of strangulation to Melissa that morning, in actual fact in the script, Becky dies from a gunshot wound. While Damian's in the bathroom after proposing, a man comes in, shoots all the people in the restaurant, and leaves. There are no witnesses to the crime and no apparent motive. Becky's death launches the rest of Damian's life in ways that frankly I don't care about, since I'm not in the rest of the film. The point is that, after we film Damian leaving for the bathroom, the focus is on the death scene, meaning me.

"As I've spoken of briefly, we aren't filming the death itself. The movie is from Damian's perspective, so there are no shots without his presence. Therefore, bang, bang, you've been shot, Gracie. Melissa…" Ben pauses.

"Yes, Benjamin."

"Make Gracie look like she's been shot."

"Will do."

Two hours later, after lying still on the floor in a "blood" stained dress as a corpse, I am ready to be finished. It turns out that it *is* kind of creepy to play a dead woman.

"Thanks, Ben," I say, taking the offered cheek. I've cleaned up and am saying my final good byes. "I had a blast working with you guys. I'm sure the rest of filming will be great. I can't wait for the finished film." Hugs all around and then, as I'm headed for the door…

"Watch out for dark alleys."

Ben looks confused, Melissa rolls her eyes, and Sam has vanished again.

"You know I will, Adam," I say with breezy confidence and exit the scene. All the way home, though, I keep hearing Adam's earlier comment running crazily in my head.

I'm sure he won't be waiting for you when we finish filming today.

CHAPTER TWELVE

As I walk to the subway station, I run lines in my head. With Jane's help for the past few days, I have the scenes down cold for my *Heart's Home* callback. I barely register anyone around me on the street and then on the subway, as I focus inward on the dialogue. When I arrive at the studio, I am pleased to realize that all of my preparation has evidently eliminated any feelings of nervousness about callbacks. Despite my inward focus, I manage to pass through security and identify myself to the receptionist, who leads me to a small conference room down the hall from where the initial audition meeting was held.

There are already four other girls in the room. Although I am early, I am still apparently the last one to arrive. Oh, well. The receptionist leaves to get Meg Ashton, the casting director. I take the remaining empty seat on the end of a row of five chairs.

"Hi, I'm Gracie," I introduce myself to the woman seated next to me. She looks briefly startled (some people don't believe in talking to the competition), then smiles.

"I'm Elizabeth. Nice to meet you."

"You, too. Have you been waiting long?"

"No, I only got here a minute before you." Elizabeth appears like she maybe wants to say something more, but Meg arrives.

"Hello, ladies. How are you this morning?" A chorus of fines greets the question. "Great. I assume all of you read the character description, along with memorizing the dialogue." A murmur of assent from us. "Good. Then let's jump right in. You five are the remaining contenders and one of you *will* get the part."

The energy level in the room rises on that statement.

"The part of Janie is a long-lost sister to Max, one of our most popular characters. She's slated to be in town for about a month, helping to plan and execute their great-grandmother Lily's 100th birthday party celebration. Naturally, this being a daytime drama, things do not go as smoothly as planned." Meg smiles widely and we dutifully chuckle. It wouldn't be on a soap opera if it went as planned.

"There is a small sound room next door. I'm going to have each of you do the three partial scenes with Richard Garcia, the actor who plays Max. That's it. Any questions?" There weren't. "You'll audition in the order you arrived. I believe that makes Felicia first?" Felicia follows Meg out of the room. The four of us remaining wait in silence. No more small talk, I guess.

Felicia returns about ten minutes later and Dana follows Meg to the room next door. Interestingly, Felicia does not leave, but instead takes her seat. I'm dying of curiosity, as I'm sure the other women are, and still nobody says anything. I'll find out soon enough, I decide, picking a spot on the far wall to maintain focus while I continue to run lines in my head.

After Dana, Judith, and Elizabeth are finished, it is finally my turn. I follow Meg into the hallway.

"It's good to see you, Gracie."

"You, too, Meg."

"Any difficulty with the memorization?"

"Nope. My roommate helped me," I answer as we enter another room. There are three chairs, one of which is occupied by an indeterminately ethnic-looking man, and a camera. I notice the camera is not set up to film the individuals who would be seated in the chairs, nor does it, in fact, even seem to be on. As Meg and I sit in the unoccupied seats, she answers my unasked questions.

"Due to the fast-track nature of the audition, I won't be filming the callbacks. After you've auditioned, Richard and I will discuss the five of you, and somebody will be offered the part this morning."

"Wow, that's fast." And highly unusual.

"The plan is for the character to be introduced in next week's filming, so we need our actress basically to sign a contract right now."

"Makes sense," I agree, eager to show her that I'm the right actress to sign that contract. Meg introduces Richard and me to each other, we shake hands, and then we're off to the races. The first partial scene has a happy overall tone, the second is angry, and the third is sad. I do my best to not play any of them as one-note. At the end, I even manage to squeeze out a single tear. When we finish, I am ready for my Emmy award.

"That was wonderful," Meg says.

"You really nailed it," Richard agrees.

"Thanks. It just feels natural to me."

"That definitely came across," Richard comments.

Meg rises and I follow suit. "If you'll wait in the conference room with the others, and tell them we'll make our decision shortly," Meg says, opening the door. I walk back to the conference room, practically with a bounce in my step. I just know I am getting the part.

"Meg says she'll be with us shortly, to tell us her decision," I inform the other women as I enter the conference room and head for my seat. Several of the women nod and smile, but still nobody says anything.

After what feels like an hour, but was really about ten minutes, the door to the conference room opens and Meg and Richard enter together and approach the five of us. We're on the edge of our seats, waiting with bated breath, choose your expression. We want to know the decision.

"First of all, let me tell you how wonderful all of you were. This was really a tough decision. When it came down to finally choosing, the choice was clear. Gracie," Meg says and looks at me. "Congratulations, you got the part of Janie."

While my adrenaline shoots through the stratosphere at the news, I am aware of the disappointment of the other actresses. I therefore contain myself as best as I can. "Thank you so much," I enthuse to Meg and Richard as the other women thank Meg for the opportunity to audition and leave the room. After the other women have gone, I become the sole focus in the room.

"Congratulations again," Meg tells me.

"You really were the clear choice, sis," Richard says with a smile before leaving.

"Thanks," I call after him.

"Now that the fun and games are over, let's get down to business."

"What do you need from me, Meg?"

"We've got contracts to sign and I have a script for you to memorize."

"Sounds wonderful."

I follow Meg back to her office where we settle all the business details, faxing back and forth to Catherine as well (an agent's gotta earn her percentage, after all). Meg hands me my script, instructs me when and where to be for filming next week, and I am out the door. All of this before lunch.

I am flying so high on excitement that I don't immediately recognize Average Guy when I arrive at my apartment building. He and another man follow me into the lobby.

"I'm simply crushed," comes a familiar voice from behind. My good mood evaporates when I see who has spoken. I say nothing and he continues. "Don't tell me you don't remember me?" he asks with mock indignation.

"I remember you," I say flatly, but with a sliver of fear.

"Oh, good, that will make this easier."

"What do you want?" I am suddenly curious and, strangely, no longer afraid.

Tommy aka Average Guy seems to sense my mood change.

"We just want to talk to you about… things," Creepy Guy in a seersucker suit says.

"He speaks," I reply with attitude.

"Now, now, there's no need for attitude," Tommy insists. "This can all be amicable."

"What are you, the mob? Is the Godfather gonna put a cap in my ass?" My bravado is wonderful; when am I going to learn to keep my mouth shut? Probably never.

"You shouldn't joke about matters you don't understand," Creepy Guy says, with what he probably imagines is a knowing, subtly threatening tone of voice. What is it with these guys?

"You're not really with the mob, are you?" I ask, suddenly sure of the answer.

They exchange a look.

"Are you part of a drug cartel? Or something smaller?"

"We're like, an affiliate," Tommy says. I can't help it, but I laugh. They look non-plussed.

"So, you're like the junior mob or the baby mob?" Uh-oh, Creepy Guy is doing a better job looking menacing. The sliver of fear returns with a vengeance. "Not that it matters," I quickly attempt to backpedal. I need to get this situation under control before the fear becomes unmanageable. "I haven't seen or heard anything that would ever be repeated in polite society."

The goons smile. "See that you don't," Tommy says. And, just like that, they're gone.

With their absence, I notice the fear has now gone as well. My smart mouth pops open.

"Wait," I call out into the empty lobby. "Do you consider the police department polite society?"

CHAPTER THIRTEEN

"Congrats on being cast," Jane says distractedly. "But, really, you're your own soap opera."

"Don't I know it." I have just finished telling her what happened in the lobby.

"What next?"

"I begin filming on Monday."

"That's not what I meant."

"I know." I sigh dramatically. "I thought I'd just pretend I didn't see anything. That way I don't end up dead – or with broken kneecaps."

"You can't be serious!" Jane looks horrified that I wouldn't report the drug deal and the veiled threats to the authorities now that I know the identity of the dealer.

"I'm not," I assure her, sighing again, though less dramatically.

Jane throws a pillow at me.

"I've spent the last few hours deciding what to say and figuring out where I should go," I explain.

"Yeah?"

"Yeah. There's a local police station just a few blocks from here. I figure I'll walk in tomorrow morning and ask to speak to someone about drugs… and possibly organized crime."

"What do you think the dealer will do?" Jane looks nervous now.

"I'm hoping that the cops will be able to handle it in such a way that he can't conclusively prove it was me."

"Um… you do know he can kill you without conclusive proof, right?"

"Of course. My hope is that he won't be too eager to engage in murder if he isn't certain I spoke."

"Why would he care one way or the other?"

"He's a dealer, not a killer."

"You know this, how?"

"I don't, for sure. But, he was the advance man for his boss's business interests. I doubt the boss would want such a visible employee to engage in permanent solutions to problems," I point out with supreme confidence.

"I guess that makes sense," Jane reluctantly agrees.

"Anyway, I'm going to the cops first thing in the morning."

Jane unexpectedly laughs.

"What?"

"Your life really is a soap opera – affair with a married man; crazy, drug-addict, jealous wife; threatening drug-dealing goon. Your life has it all."

"Never a dull moment," I agree with a smile.

CHAPTER FOURTEEN

I feel like I could jump out of my skin while walking to the police station. Why, you may wonder? Perhaps it's because I'm about to report a man for illegal activities. A man (and his goon friend) who may just want to kill me, or at least hurt me, for the effort. It's natural to be nervous under these circumstances, one would think.

The blocks pass without notice or incident. I've stopped and am urging my legs to move, but my brain is ineffectual. I'm across the street from the police station. Officers enter and exit, civilians do the same, nobody pays anybody else any mind.

What if someone followed me? What if I am being watched? My paranoid thoughts run wild, imagining a multitude of scenarios, none of which end well for me.

Stop! I internally command myself and attempt to look around me in as surreptitious a manner as I can. I feel completely exposed but, as far as I can see anyway, nobody seems to care one whit about me standing here.

I try again to convince my legs to move forward and, miracle of miracles, they do. I walk with much more confidence than I honestly feel. I arrive at the door to the police station. It magically opens, as though issuing me an invitation to enter. Okay, so it wasn't really magic.

"Thank you," I say with a smile to the uniformed officer who opened the door for me.

"You're welcome, miss," he replies, smiling in return. In this instant, I know I am doing the right thing and I stop him in the doorway.

"Where do I go to report a crime?"

The officer points to a ruddy-faced heavy-set older gentleman behind a counter. "The desk sergeant will be happy to assist you."

"Great, thanks." With a final smile, I enter the station. I walk with purpose toward the desk sergeant.

"How can I help you?"

"I'd like to report a crime, possibly two crimes." Is a veiled death threat a crime in this state? Focus, Gracie.

"Tell me what happened," the sergeant encourages me.

"I witnessed what looked like a drug deal and wasn't going to say anything, but then, by chance, I ran into the guy while I was working – I'm an actress – and he recognized me, too. He and another guy came to my home and in not-so-many-words threatened me if I went to the authorities. Which I decided to do anyway," I finish with determination. I've said all of this in one breath and now abruptly stop for the sergeant's response.

"That's quite a story," is all he says, while he picks up his phone and dials a number. "You busy?" He directs this question to the phone. "I have someone here who should talk to you." He listens for a moment and hangs up. "Vincent King will be up here in a minute. He's a narcotics detective," he explains before I can ask.

"Thank you very much. Where should I wait?" The sergeant directs me vaguely down the length of the room just as a youngish Italian-looking man in blue jeans and a black tee shirt steps through a door. Our eyes meet. He strides purposefully to me. I do the same.

"Vincent King. Are you the person I'm looking for?"

"Absolutely. I'm Gracie Corsini and I have information about drugs and baby mobsters."

Detective King had already turned to go back through the door, but he pauses in the doorway. "Baby mobsters?" His eyes are questioning.

"Oh, sorry. That'll make more sense after I tell you my story," I assure him and we continue through the door.

The detective and I wind our way through a veritable maze of desks and cubicles. The level of activity around us is incredible. We arrive at a desk that appears to be his.

"Please, have a seat," he says, unfailingly polite as he indicates the chair opposite his desk.

I take the offered seat and am inexplicably nervous again as I prepare to tell my story to an actual professional crime fighter. What if he laughs me out of the station? Detective King is watching me and I wonder how my emotions must be playing out across my face.

"Why don't you start at the beginning?" He has a pad of paper and pen at the ready to record all pertinent information. Or, maybe he'll just doodle.

"Okay," I say while I organize the sequence of events in my mind. When I'm satisfied that I have all of the details and timeline recalled, I tell Detective King about Tommy Pullman and the goon in the seersucker suit. I notice some kind of nonverbal reaction when I say Tommy's name, but otherwise the detective simply scribbles while I talk.

"That's an interesting story," he offers blandly when I finish my tale.

"What happens now?"

"I can tell you we have an ongoing investigation into Mr. Pullman and his associates," the detective begins. "We're hoping to flip Mr. Pullman – have him give us his boss."

"Does that mean my information can be more like collateral?" I interrupt, using my movie- and television-generated knowledge. "You know, so you can call me a confidential informant and I can keep my kneecaps?"

Detective King smiles at my questions. "Ms. Corsini, we will do everything we can to keep you safe."

Although that's not really an answer, it still makes me feel better. "What's next then?"

"For now, just sit tight. Let us continue our investigation and when we need you, we'll call. Most likely, the most we'll want is for you to come back and make a formal statement regarding the events that occurred. Right now, however, we'll just put your information in the context of what information we've been gathering in our investigation to date."

Most of that sounds like double-speak to me, but I figure I'm not going to get anything else. I stand up to leave.

"Thank you very much for taking the time to listen to me."

"You're welcome. Thank you for coming in with your story. Not everyone would do that."

I smile and, with a nod, turn to leave, glad that he chose not to highlight the fact that I didn't come in after witnessing the drug deal, but rather, waited until my own personal safety was threatened. Just a typical self-absorbed person, I think with a sigh as I exit the station. At least it's over for a while.

I have my first day of filming on the soap opera tomorrow.

CHAPTER FIFTEEN

Despite the time being earlier than the ass-crack of dawn, I wake up before the dulcet chirping of my cell phone alarm. I shower, dress, and grab a quick bite to eat before heading to the studio. I'm feeling great until I hit security. Why is my heart suddenly racing?

I place my backpack on the conveyor belt through the scanner and walk through the metal detector. I get through security without incident and George, the security guard, congratulates me on being cast and points where I should go.

I cannot believe how nervous I am. I've been completely fine until this point. I arrive at a dressing room I'll be sharing with a couple of other recurring characters and seeing my name on the door relaxes me.

"You can do this," I say aloud.

"Of course, you can," comes the response behind me. I feel my face flush with embarrassment as I turn around.

"Hi, Meg. Just giving myself a little pep talk."

"That's only natural," Meg insists, laughing off my embarrassment. "Everyone gets nervous, but if they've prepared, they do fine." I nod and she continues. "Was your roommate able to run lines with you again?"

"Yes. She's been great. She says she's having fun doing it, so she's promised to continue throughout the time I'm on the show."

"Wonderful. Don't forget my offer, though."

"I won't," I promise.

"I can easily have an intern or PA read lines with you," she reminds me. "It would almost be like having an assistant," Meg jokes.

"Thanks for the offer. I'll definitely take you up on it if Jane can't do it, if it becomes any kind of problem or burden," I assure Meg. She nods and quickly walks away. Now that's a woman who knows where she's going.

I enter the dressing room and take a seat at a mirror. The absence of knickknacks or other territorial announcements informs me this section is unoccupied. One thing I've learned is that women can be quite competitive about mirror space. I set my backpack down and survey my surroundings. There are five other chairs, lots of scattered belongings, and two racks of clothing at the far end of the room. I decide to find my wardrobe.

My scenes today basically involve my introduction as a character, including meeting a few soap town notables. There's a section of one clothing rack labeled with my name and I see a number of different pieces. As I paw through, I note jeans with a red tee shirt, and a khaki skirt with a pink button-down top. At that moment, a production assistant pops into the room.

"They need you at hair and makeup. Come with me, I can take you."

"Thanks. First day," I explain.

"Yeah, I know. That's why I offered to show you," the production assistant says. Her expression is inscrutable.

"Oh, right. Well, thanks."

I follow the unnamed woman with her icy blond hair and flat attitude to hair and makeup, wondering if maybe really she's an unhappy, unpaid intern. My first scene takes place at the home of my brother and his family, shortly after I've stepped off the plane. Hair and makeup are kept quite simple. There's some talk amongst the crew, but everything seems tense and like barely-controlled chaos.

Back in the dressing room, changing into the jeans and tee shirt, I reflect on how different the feel of this set is from anything I've ever done before. I decide finally to say screw it and run lines in my head until I'm called to the set.

I can't remember walking there, but I am standing on set watching the crew work and wondering where the hell the other actors are.

"Hey, Gracie," says a familiar male voice behind me.

"Hi, Richard," I'm already replying as I turn around. Finally, a familiar, friendly face.

"It's good to see you."

"It's good to see you, too. I was beginning to wonder if I'd gotten the date of filming wrong," I joke.

"Yeah, it is kinda quiet today. We're the only ones in the first scene, but a whole bunch more people will be arriving in," he checks his watch, "about an hour or so, for the later scenes. We try to stagger call times as much as we can, so we don't have actors wandering around bored any more than we have to," Richard explains.

"That makes sense," I comment, feeling like an idiot that it hadn't occurred to me. Guess I'm still nervous.

Richard and I chat for maybe another fifteen minutes before a harried-looking woman heads in our direction.

"Hi, Richard. You, I assume, are Graciella," the woman addresses us.

"Yes, I'm Gracie."

"Hi, Miranda," Richard greets the woman.

"Gracie, I'm the director, Miranda Borden. Are you ready to begin?"

"Absolutely."

"For this scene, I want the two of you seated on the couch to start," Miranda begins. "You've just gotten in from the airport and you and your brother are catching up. As you move through the dialogue, be as expressive as you think Janie would be, but remain seated for this first run-through. Okay?"

"Got it." My mind swirls with the possibilities for the scene.

"Richard?"

"I'm ready."

Miranda has us run through the scene several times, once sitting down, once standing up, and once as a combination. Then we do a couple of mid-, short-, and close-ups and we're done.

"That was great, guys," Miranda comments as we wrap the scene. "By the way, Gracie, welcome aboard." She smiles.

"Thanks," I reply, mirroring her smile. "I'm glad to be here."

"Take thirty while we set for the dinner scene," the director instructs. She's off to work out logistics and I turn to Richard.

"That was fast," I say in amazement.

"When you have to get out five hours of show every week, you don't tend to spend much time on any one scene," he explains.

"No kidding. It's so different from the double-digit numbers of takes in film."

"You seem to have adapted well," Richard compliments me.

"Thanks."

"It's even more important on a soap set than any other to really know your lines solid and to hit your mark every time."

"Of course," I agree.

"You did that just fine for your first scene. I could tell that Miranda was pleased."

"Oh, good."

"There's always a slight worry that a new actor will underestimate the challenge of working in daytime."

"I could see that happening. I just hope I can do as well in the next scene."

Richard puts his hand on my shoulder in a comforting gesture. "You'll do fine."

"Thanks. I better go change into my new outfit."

With that, we head off in opposite directions. Arriving in my dressing room, there are now three other women in varying stages of readiness.

"You must be Janie," a redhead with blue eyes and freckles addresses me immediately.

"Yep," I say with a chuckle. "You can call me Gracie."

"I'm Danielle, playing Chrissie."

"I'm Kris," a blond struggling into a crazy-tight skirt introduces herself. "I play Bella."

"And I'm Megan," the final woman in the room, also blond, introduces herself. "I play Robin."

"It's nice to meet all of you." The women echo that sentiment as I walk over to my clothing so I can change for the next scene.

"How's it going so far?" Danielle asks.

"My first-day jitters have settled and Richard said the first scene went well."

"I'm off to the set," Megan announces to the room as she exits.

"Richard's a great guy. Honest, too. If he says it went well, you can trust that," Danielle assures me.

"That's good to know." Having removed the jeans and tee shirt, I place them on their hangers.

"We're off to the set, too," Danielle says, as she and Kris rise to leave.

"It was nice to meet you, Gracie," Kris says again as they depart.

As I slip into the khakis and button-down top, I'm feeling great. The first scene went well. I met some of the other actresses and they seem nice. "Let's bring it home," I tell my reflection before heading to the set myself.

Arriving on set, the makeup artist immediately descends upon me to both darken and freshen my makeup from the earlier scene. Then, the hair stylist magically appears, pulling various strands of hair around my face. Satisfied with the result, she melts away.

The previous scene was set in a house, so the set looked like a standard living room. This next scene occurs in a restaurant and, except for the missing ceiling, I could be standing in your average family dining establishment. There are already people seated around some of the tables. Not being familiar with the show, I have no idea initially who are the extras and who are in the main cast. All I know is that it is during this scene that my 'brother' introduces me to others in 'town'.

"Gracie, I'd like you to sit here," Miranda directs me to a central table. As I do, she continues. "Richard, good, you're here. Please sit there, next to Gracie." I crane my head around to see Richard striding toward the table. He takes his seat.

"You ready, Gracie?"

"You know it, Richard."

An increase in the room noise distracts me. From my experience as an extra, I know that the murmuring signals the presence of a lead actor. Again, I crane my head around. I don't immediately recognize him, as I'd only seen him before in commercials for his movie and in snippets on entertainment shows. Instead, his incredible good looks mesmerize me.

"He gets that reaction a lot," Richard comments dryly.

"What?" I'm distracted from my ogling.

"You made a little noise in your throat," he explains.

"I did?"

"Yep. And he gets that a lot."

"I'm sure he does," I agree, my attention focused again on the hot actor. Julian. Suddenly, his name bubbles to the surface of my mind. Julian McNamara. He is the soap star who left to do a movie, it tanked, and now he's back. Judging by the reactions of others on the set, he must not have returned too long ago. For the scene, he's dressed in upscale casual and I'm admiring the fit of the clothes when our eyes meet.

Julian's expressive brown eyes fix on mine for so long that a couple of other people glance in my direction. He tilts his head and smiles, revealing beautiful, perfectly white teeth. I smile back a split second before someone draws his attention away and he breaks his gaze.

"Damn," I utter. I could feel the electricity between us from across the room.

"I'll say," Richard agrees.

I look at him quizzically.

"Snap, crackle, and pop," he says with a knowing look.

"You could feel it, huh?"

"Honey, everyone in the building could feel that. You do know he's married, right?"

"Absolutely," I answer, but evidently without much conviction. Richard appears concerned. "It's not a problem," I assert.

"Staying away from him or ignoring the fact that he's married?" Richard asks with a smirk.

"Funny guy," I respond and don't answer the question.

Richard's eyes focus over my shoulder and I sense a presence.

"Hello, Richard," comes a voice from behind me.

"Hi, Julian," Richard replies.

Before I do anything, Julian has taken an empty seat at our table. "I don't believe we've met," Julian states.

"No, we haven't. Today's my first day. I'm Gracie."

"It's nice to meet you, Gracie. Welcome to the show." He offers his hand and I accept it. Hot damn! The electricity between us is palpable. I'm speechless, but saved from having to speak by the director.

"C'mon, Julian. That's enough of making the new girl feel welcome."

"Okay, okay," Julian teases. "We'll talk later," he tells me before following the director back to his table.

"This should be interesting."

I sigh. "Look, Richard. I am not getting involved with a married man. I don't care how much snap, crackle, and pop is between us," I stress.

"Good to hear. I'd hate to see my new co-star get hurt."

That's the end of the conversation, as Miranda begins the shoot. It goes well. There are restaurant crowd shots at first, then individual bits at the few tables with main characters. I am pleased to report that I don't flub a single line. By lunchtime, we're finished filming my stuff. Just as I'm wondering what to do next, the production assistant with the icy blond hair approaches.

"Here are your pages for the next two weeks," she says, handing me a sheaf of papers. "You aren't called again until Thursday, but then it's everyday thereafter." Her look asks if I understand, so I nod. She turns and walks away. I am standing there wondering if it's me she doesn't like, if it's everyone she doesn't like, or if she's just having a really bad day, when I sense an already familiar presence behind me. I turn before he speaks.

"Gracie."

"Julian." Awkward, awkward, awkward.

"How was your first day?" Julian finally asks.

"It was great," I answer, too enthusiastically. The man makes me so nervous. "Everyone's been nice... and welcoming." I stop abruptly.

"That's good. We're a friendly bunch, so I would expect nothing less."

"Are you filming the rest of the day?" I am not sure what to say to this man. I absolutely do not want him to think I'm flirting. But, the attraction between us is distracting.

"Yes. Ever since I came back, they've been working me to the bone," Julian says with a laugh.

"That just means they like you."

"I certainly hope so," he agrees. "When do you come back?"

Warning bells go off in my head. His question seems like a veiled *When can I see you again?* "Um, Thursday." Besides, doesn't he have a script?

"Maybe we'll bump into each other between scenes, since we don't have any together."

"Maybe," I respond slowly. "I should get going. You don't want to waste your whole lunch break talking to me."

"It wouldn't be a waste." He smiles and I smile automatically in return.

"Okay, see you Thursday." With that, I turn away from Julian and begin walking toward the dressing room. I can feel his eyes on me.

I practically collapse in my chair in the dressing room. Filming for the next month is going to be interesting. I know I can stay strong and not succumb to his charms, but I also know it may be akin to torture.

The instant I exit the building, I dial my phone.

"You busy?"

"Nah," Jane answers. "How was your first day of filming?"

"Depends."

"Uh-oh. On what?"

"On what aspect of the filming day."

Jane starts laughing.

"What?"

"Who is he?"

"What makes you think there's a guy involved?"

"Who is he?" Jane asks again.

"Julian McNamara," I answer with a sigh.

"Wait. Do I know him? The name sounds familiar."

"He's the most popular actor on *Heart's Home* right now. He had that movie earlier that flopped."

"That's right. Hey, isn't he married?"

"Hmm-mm."

"Oh," Jane says with dawning understanding. "Therein lies the problem."

"You got it."

"What happened? Did you do something already?"

"Of course not. Number one, it's my first day. Number two, he's a married co-worker."

"Is the problem you might do something?"

"No. The problem is that I might want to do something every time I see him."

"You just met him. You sound like a teenage girl."

"Thanks, Jane. Way to be supportive," I respond dryly. "The chemistry between us was so strong that Richard even commented on it."

"Richard is the guy who plays your brother?"

"Right."

"What did he say?"

"Snap, crackle, and pop."

Jane bursts into laughter.

"Again, I have to say, not very supportive."

"Sorry," Jane says, not sounding very sorry. "You have to admit, that's funny."

"Yeah," I agree with a smile.

"Are you on your way home?"

"Walking to the subway now."

"You got a call from someone in the DA's office while I was in the shower. She wants you to call her."

"Okay. Thanks for the heads up."

"See you at the house."

"See ya."

I continue to head for home, on autopilot now because my head is swirling. Not with thoughts of Julian, but of gangsters and dismembered body parts. God, I hope I didn't make a mistake coming forward.

"Hello, this message is for Graciella Corsini. This is Aliana Gregson, with the district attorney's office. Please give me a call at your earliest convenience. My number is 212-555-7541."

I listen to the message, thinking I was right to give Detective King my home line rather than my cell phone number. I could dodge the district attorney indefinitely if I chose to. With another sigh (I seem to be doing that a lot lately), I dial the number on my cell phone.

"May I speak to Aliana Gregson, please?" I ask the receptionist who answers.

"This is Aliana Gregson," a woman says after the receptionist transfers the call.

"This is Graciella Corsini, returning your call."

"Ms. Corsini, thank you for getting back to me so quickly. I was calling regarding information you provided to Detective Vincent King."

"Yes?"

"The district attorney's office plans to move forward against Thomas Pullman."

"Detective King gave me the impression that Tommy was going to be – what's the term? – flipped, to testify against his boss. And my involvement would cease," I stress that last sentence.

"Mr. Pullman declined to cooperate because he does not seem to believe we have a case. He doesn't think our witness, in particular, will testify against him."

"You mean me," I state.

"Yes. Without Mr. Pullman, we don't have a strong enough case against his boss. We've decided to convene a grand jury to hopefully indict Mr. Pullman on multiple charges, some of which stem from your encounters with him. We hope that when he appreciates the severity of the charges against him, he will change his mind about helping us."

"If he does, then my involvement ends with the grand jury?"

"Yes."

"And if he doesn't, then I'll likely have to testify against Tommy in court?"

"That's correct."

"You are aware that Tommy and an associate basically threatened to kill me, right?"

"Yes, I am."

"What's being done about that?"

"After the grand jury indicts Mr. Pullman, we can either take you into protective custody, or provide you with protection."

"Oh, my," is all I can think to say.

"It's your decision whether or not to cooperate, of course," Ms. Gregson begins. "I can only ask you to consider what happens if you don't. Nothing will change in the organization and Mr. Pullman still might not leave you alone."

"Yeah, I thought about all of that. You don't have to worry. I'm on board. Just tell me when and where I need to be."

"The grand jury meets tomorrow."

"That's fast."

"We don't want to sit on this any longer than necessary."

"Works for me."

The remainder of the conversation consists of Ms. Gregson telling me the location of the courthouse and my expected time of arrival. When I hang up the phone, I decide I need a movie to put myself in the mood to go to court tomorrow.

As I walk the block to the video store (yes, they still exist), I find myself watching every person I pass, occasionally glancing behind me, and just generally acting paranoid. Of course, as they say, it's not paranoia if someone is really out to get you.

In my vigilance, I see nothing out of the ordinary and I make it back to my apartment in one piece. I pop the movie, *Legally Blond*, into the DVD player and sit back to watch Reese Witherspoon rock the legal world. Jane arrives home from work in time to watch the daughter confess to her father's murder and sits down to watch the last few minutes of the film.

"That is a great movie," I enthuse when the end credits begin to role.

"Yes it is," Jane agrees. "What triggered the rental?"

"I spoke to the woman in the DA's office and I'm going before the grand jury tomorrow."

Jane's eyes widen. "I thought you weren't really going to be involved."

I recount my conversation with Aliana Gregson.

"Are you going to take their protection?"

"Well, I'm certainly not going into protective custody. I just landed the biggest break of my career."

"It won't do you much good if you're dead."

"True, but that's why I decided I'll take the bodyguard option."

"Do you think he'll be hot? I've seen the movies. Hot bodyguard protects beautiful actress… sex always follows."

"I don't know about all that," I respond between laughs. "I think I'm gonna run the movie back to the store, so I don't have to tomorrow before court."

"Do you want me to go with you?"

"That's sweet, but it's only a block and I doubt Tommy has heard yet that I'll be at the grand jury tomorrow."

"Do you even know how this works?"

"Well, no, but on TV it's only when they go to trial that there are witness lists and advance notice."

"If it happens that way on TV, then it must be accurate."

I throw my crumpled video store receipt at Jane and head for the door. "I'll be fine. I'll be right back."

The return trip to the video store is again uneventful. I slide my movie in the slot and begin walking back toward my apartment building. I make it almost to my building when…

"Hey, Gracie."

The familiar voice freezes me. I immediately note the presence of several other people on the sidewalk and feel reasonably confident that he isn't planning to kill me. At least not right here, right now. I turn to face him.

"Hi, Tommy."

"I hear there's a party tomorrow and you're the star," Tommy says cryptically.

"If there is a party tomorrow, I'm sure there's a festive occasion inspiring it."

"Cut the crap, Gracie."

"You started it, Tommy." Wow, that's mature.

"I thought we had an understanding."

"I don't know what you're talking about."

"Sure you do," Tommy disagrees in a low threatening tone.

The fear that is unfortunately becoming all too familiar begins blossoming. All of this adrenaline cannot be good for my system. I decide the best response is to flee. "No, I really don't,"

I say, with a sense of assertiveness I definitely do not feel, then turn to go.

"We're not finished here," Tommy says in that same low voice, reaching out a hand to grab my elbow.

"Yes, we are," I respond in an equally low voice, the fear expanding exponentially. I decide I need the possibility of reinforcements. "Let go of me," I continue, much louder, attracting the attention of passers-by.

Tommy lets go and raises his hands in mock surrender. "No need to get upset. We're just talking here."

"No, we're not. We're done," I tell him with finality. He looks furious but continues to smile. I turn and walk away, half-tensed, waiting for him to stop me with his voice, his hand, or a bullet. None of those things happen and I walk into my apartment building as I have a thousand times before. I take the stairs two at a time and get to the apartment breathless.

"What happened?" Jane asks this as soon as I step into the apartment.

I sit on the couch, put my head between my legs, and wait for the vertigo to pass.

"What happened?" Jane asks again, sounding alarmed.

"In a minute," I mumble from between my legs and miraculously Jane waits without quizzing me further. After several minutes I feel level enough to sit up. Jane still does not repeat her question, waiting for me to be ready.

"I ran into everybody's favorite life-threatening drug dealer on my way back from the video store," I start.

"Oh, my God."

"As you can see, nothing happened."

"This time," Jane corrects me.

"Well, whatever. After tomorrow, I'll have protection."

"Doesn't that mean he's more likely to try something tonight or tomorrow morning?"

"I don't think so."

"Why not?"

"I'm thinking he might believe the confrontation alone will scare me out of going to court tomorrow."

"You think?"

"Yeah, I do."

"Well," Jane sighs, "I certainly hope you're right. All I know is, I won't be sleeping a wink until that man is behind bars."

"Amen," I agree wholeheartedly.

CHAPTER SIXTEEN

After a sleepless night and several cups of coffee, I feel like I'm having an out-of-body experience. That, or my skin is trying to peel itself off of my skeleton. Despite the jitters, I manage to look presentable when I leave my apartment.

With every step, I feel an insane urge to peek over my shoulder. I know, I know, I told Jane that I didn't think Tommy would try anything before the grand jury. And, I don't, not really. But, the survival instinct is strong and this morning it is singing hosannas in my brain.

My travel to the courthouse by sidewalk and subway remains trauma-free. Thirty minutes before my scheduled time, I find myself across the street from the entrance. I flashback to the day not so long ago when I found myself in a similar situation before entering the police station. Then, as now, I take a deep breath and, with full confidence in myself and my choice, I start across the street.

"Hey lady! Watch where you're walking!"

Oh, good job, Gracie. I raise my hand in a *mea culpa* at the taxi driver who yelled at me.

"Sorry," I holler back and scurry the remaining way across the street. Without any more thoughts of angry gangsters and feeling grateful the taxi didn't squash me, I enter the building.

The foyer of the building is more majestic than I would have imagined any building connected to the civil service would be – but it truly is almost cavernous, with soaring ceilings and a hushed, library-like atmosphere. I walk to a circular desk with a large <u>Information</u> sign suspended above.

"I'm here for a grand jury," I begin. "I'm presenting information, testifying," I clarify, not wanting her to think I'm a jury member.

"Go through Security to the right and follow the signs. Look for the suits. That means you've found the lawyers," the woman explains with a smile.

"Thank you very much." Who says civil servants are surly? Of course, she could be a volunteer.

At Security, I hand my purse to a guard for inspection while I pass through the metal detector. No alarm sounds and the security guard returns my belongings. I walk down the hallway to the right, quickly spotting Grand Jury Room signs. After a few twists and turns, I run into a horde of suits. Ah, lawyers. I must be close to my destination.

"Excuse me," I tap a woman (Puerto Rican, maybe?) on the shoulder. "I'm looking for Aliana Gregson."

"You've found me. Are you Graciella Corsini?"

"Yes, I am."

"How are you doing this morning?"

I sense this is not asked simply to be polite. "To be completely honest, I'm a little nervous," I admit.

"I'd be worried if you weren't," Ms. Gregson tells me, I assume to make me feel better. It does, a bit. "Today is going to be mostly boring, though."

"Really?"

"Believe it or not," she answers with a nod. "You can't be in the room until it's your turn, so you'll spend that time in a holding area."

Like a celebrity waiting in the green room before an appearance, I think, but don't say. "Do you have an idea how long this will take?"

"It can really vary. If you plan for the day, you'll be happy if we finish earlier."

I can tell this is a line she's had considerable practice giving, but it makes sense. It's sort of like on a cattle call audition. Ms. Gregson takes my silence as an assent and continues.

"If you'll follow me, I'll show you where the room is and where the restrooms are."

"That's always the most important."

"Definitely," she agrees as we make our way a short distance down another adjacent hallway. "Here we are," she announces, opening a nondescript door without any indication of the room's use. Entering the room, I note two wooden tables with uncomfortable-looking chairs encircling them. At least there is a window, although it overlooks a parking garage.

"Thanks," I say, just to say something, as I set my purse on the table.

"You're welcome. Thank you for agreeing to appear before the grand jury." I nod. "Oh, and the chairs are much more comfortable than they look." I smile at the comment and Ms. Gregson departs.

"Where is everybody else?" I wonder aloud as it sinks in that I'm now in this room alone. Could the prosecutor really have no other witnesses? As if in response to my questions, the door opens and two gentlemen in suits appear.

"Ms. Corsini?" A portly older gentleman with white hair and matching beard asks this question. I suspect he gets asked to play Santa Claus every Christmas season.

"Yes," I affirm and stand up from the chair in which I had just taken a seat. Ms. Gregson was right; it was much more comfortable than it looked.

"I am Assistant District Attorney Leonard Myers. This is my paralegal, Jackson Goram."

I was walking as he introduced himself and his colleague, and now I offer my hand as I approach. "It's nice to meet you both."

"I wanted to let you know that you will be testifying first."

"So there are others," I interrupt with my implied question.

"Yes, but most of the others will be discussing more circumstantial aspects of the evidence related to our case. You are an actual eyewitness to crimes committed by Mr. Pullman."

"A crime," I correct.

"Actually," Mr. Myers says with a condescending smile, "his threat against you could constitute a second crime, namely intimidating a witness."

"Oh," I say, revising my earlier internal thought. This man is too smug to play Santa. "Guess we can tell who went to law school," I respond flippantly. Mr. Myers' expression does not change, but the paralegal responds with a genuine smile that he quickly loses, lest his boss see.

I don't think to ask where these other people are waiting and the men leave. Maybe the others are arriving later, like on the soap set? I play the waiting game – very boring in such a bland, empty room – for only an hour before Ms. Gregson appears in the doorway.

"Ms. Corsini, they're ready for you."

I feel an adrenaline surge as I rise and follow her out of the room, down the hallways, back to the grand jury room door.

"Ready?"

"As I'll ever be."

Ms. Gregson opens the door and motions me past her. The room looks much like what I've seen on television, so I have an idea where to go even before Mr. Myers directs me to an empty raised seat behind a podium. I find myself avoiding the eyes of the grand jury members until I take my seat. When I do look at them, it seems clear they are sizing me up.

I imagine the questions I would have if I were in their shoes. Who is she? What does she know? Can I trust her? Would she have a reason to lie? I am suddenly glad that I wore a conservative navy blue suit. I'm feeling confident and I smile at the grand jury members.

Mr. Myers jumps right in. "Please state your name for the record."

"Graciella Corsini." He asks me to spell it and I do. After a few more introductory questions, he asks a series of deeper questions to elicit every detail of the original apparent drug deal that I witnessed and the later veiled threats of Mr. Thomas Pullman and his unnamed associate. The grand jury members laugh when I use my nicknames, Skinny Guy, Average Guy, Creepy Guy, for the players involved. And, then it's finished. Since this is a grand jury proceeding, there is no defense attorney to cross-examine me. However, the grand jury members can ask questions. After a few softball, clarifying questions, a rather visually forgettable man asks me a question.

"Ms. Corsini, you stated that you first saw Mr. Pullman the night of the alleged drug deal."

"That's correct."

"Where had you been earlier in the day?"

"I was at work." Where is he going with this?

"And when you actually met Mr. Pullman and learned his identity, where were you?"

"I was at work." I thought I had already talked about this earlier…

"What is it that you do?"

"I'm an actress."

"Right. You said earlier that you learned Mr. Pullman's name when he came to your set."

"Is that a question?" This line of questioning perplexes me. I sense it isn't going to end well and I don't know why.

"I was just confirming."

"Oh, okay."

"Are you certain it was Mr. Pullman you saw in the alley?"

"Yes."

"And you're certain you never saw him before that meeting?"

"Yes."

"Is it possible that, as he later appeared at your work on a business matter, he may have other business in that neighborhood?"

"I suppose so."

"Is it possible that you had seen him before that evening?"

"No."

"You're absolutely certain that there is no way you could have ever seen him in any other context before that night?"

I hesitate. "Not that I recall." Great, now I sound wishy-washy.

"But, if you had seen him earlier than that night, isn't it possible that you saw someone who looked similar to Mr. Pullman that evening and your mind filled in the blanks with someone you had seen but did not know?"

"No." What is this guy, a defense attorney?

The grand jury member pauses as if gathering his thoughts and I wait for the next question.

"What were you filming?"

"I'm sorry?"

"You said you were an actress and you were at work before you allegedly saw Mr. Pullman and the drug deal. What were you filming?"

"Scenes in a movie."

"What scenes?"

"Relationship scenes related to later scenes of a marriage proposal and my character's murder that were to be filmed the following week." My sneak peek at the ADA shows confusion and concern on his face that I'm sure mirrors my own.

"Is it possible that filming such emotional material predisposed you to misinterpreting an exchange in a dark alleyway as something sinister?"

"Anything is possible," I respond with a shrug. "It looked like a drug deal to me," I add.

"Okay. My follow-up is related. Is it possible that after maybe witnessing a drug deal that you thought you found your drug dealer in the first man you saw who might have resembled the man you saw initially?"

"So, apparently, I either mixed him up with someone I saw before or after, but could not have been accurate in the moment?" I provide a snappish non-answer.

"Please answer the question, Ms. Corsini."

"The answer is no."

The grand jury member appears surprised at my assuredness again. "You were certain with my earlier question, too. It's not even possible?"

"No." The man looks cranky and I decide to elaborate without being asked. I don't want indictments not to follow from this proceeding because the grand jury members think I'm a bitch. "As I stated earlier, the man I saw in the alley that day stood less than a few feet away and spoke to me. When I later introduced myself to Mr. Pullman on set, he looked and sounded exactly like the man I saw. Besides, if it wasn't him, why would he threaten me later?" I ask this almost offhand, but it seems to do the trick.

"Okay, thank you." The grand jury member retakes his seat and I'm wondering if he's a plant to taint the deliberations or if he's an everyday citizen who takes his job on the grand jury very seriously.

Mr. Myers rises. "I have a follow-up question to address the concerns that were just raised. Ms. Corsini, can you tell us explicitly how you know the event you witnessed in the alley was, in fact, a drug deal?"

"I saw two men standing together. One man handed a baggy full of something to the second man in exchange for a wad of money. And, yes, before you ask, I could clearly tell it was money. There's something about a wad of money that's distinctive, you know?" I address this last to the grand jury members and exchange smiles with several. Damn, I'll make a good witness if this actually goes to trial.

"Thank you very much, Ms. Corsini."

"You're welcome." The court thanks me for my service and I leave the grand jury room. Ms. Gregson, seated on a wooden bench in the hallway, rises and approaches.

"How did it go?"

"It seemed fine. There were some unusual questions at the end from a member of the grand jury, but I think I made myself clear."

"Great. Thank you again for your assistance."

"Of course. What happens now?"

"Go on home and wait to hear from me. We have the rest of our evidence to present and then the grand jury deliberates, just like in a court trial. After they've finished, we'll find out whether or not Mr. Pullman will be indicted, or true billed, as it's called. If he is, as we hope he will be, since I understand you do not wish to be in protective custody, you will be assigned an officer for protection, pending the outcome of the case."

"Is the plan still to use the indictments to get him to flip on his boss?"

"That is the plan."

"Okay. I guess I'll go back to my apartment and wait to hear something."

"I'll call you as soon as I know anything."

"Thanks," I say as we shake hands. "Oh, wait," I tell her, fishing in my backpack for a scrap piece of paper. I scribble my cell phone number on it. Why duck the woman who might end up responsible for my safety? I hand her the paper. "If you don't reach me at home, you may have better luck with my cell," I explain.

"Thanks," Ms. Gregson replies, placing the paper inside a file she's carrying.

I walk down the hallway and back through the cavernous foyer again. I step out into the mid-morning sun, shining brightly between buildings. I eschew taking the subway and instead walk the entire distance. My walk back to the apartment is beautiful. I smile at people I pass, even saying hello to several passers-by. I should go to court more often. I feel like I've been part of something bigger than myself and it's a great feeling.

I decide to check the mail since I forgot yesterday and I'm not sure if Jane checked. As I approach, I can see the door to our box is slightly ajar. Did Jane check it and not close it securely? Did the postal carrier? The box is empty when I peer in, so I optimistically conclude that Jane must have checked it yesterday. I securely close the mailbox and head for the apartment. After entering, I look briefly for the mail as I cross the living room to my bedroom. I don't see anything. I change out of my suit into boxing shorts and a black tank top. I sit down to review my lines for tomorrow's shoot, and that's what I'm still doing when Jane arrives home.

"How was court?"

"Went well. I'm waiting to hear the results, whether or not Tommy is going to be indicted."

"When do you think you might hear something?"

"Tomorrow, maybe. The lawyer said I was at the beginning of the case, but I can't imagine there would be that much more since they seem to think I'm critical. In fact, she may have even said that they'd present the rest of their case today."

"Let me know as soon as you hear anything. Hey," Jane calls out over her shoulder as she heads for her bedroom. "Did we get any mail?"

I make a split second decision not to mention the ajar mailbox door as the name Alicia comes unbidden to my mind (although it's not out of the realm of possibility that Tommy did something). "Nah, must have been a slow mail day."

"Okay. Do you need any more help with lines? I have thirty minutes before I'm heading back to the restaurant."

"No, I'm good, thanks. Are you doing a dinner tonight?" Jane has been successfully working her way up, meaning she's increasingly getting the coveted dinner crowd.

"Yeah, Julie called in and they asked me to cover."

"Cool."

Jane clicks the television on and I disappear into my bedroom with my script. Thirty minutes later I hear the front door open and close as Jane leaves for work. After reviewing my dialogue another hour, I decide to relax watching television until I go to bed. I never give the open mailbox another thought.

*****

The next evening, I'm in my dressing room, changing out of my wardrobe from the final scene, when there's a knock on the door.

"Just a minute," I call out, hurrying to pull a cable knit top over my head. I walk over to the door and pull it open. "I was changing," I begin and trail off as I stare up into Julian's smiling brown eyes.

"My loss for knocking," he says and I ignore the comment. I will *not* flirt with this man.

"Good evening, Julian," I say cordially.

"Good evening, Graciella," he responds in the same cordial tone.

"Call me Gracie," I tell him with an internal sigh.

"Good evening, Gracie."

"What can I do for you?" Besides *do* you, my traitorous mind adds mischievously.

"I just wanted to see how you did on your filming, since we somehow missed each other all day today."

"I did fine. Thanks for checking." I smile warmly up at him – he's so tall – before I can stop myself. He responds with a full beautiful smile and I know I'm going to have a problem not falling in love with him if I keep talking to him.

"Is it true you'll be with us for only three more weeks?"

"Yep. I'm here for a month."

"That's too bad. You're a great addition." I must have a look on my face because Julian hurries to add, "As an actress, of course."

"Of course. How's your wife?"

He winces slightly before he can catch himself. I momentarily feel guilty. But, I remind myself, he's married. Heavy flirting is a no-no and helping him to remember he's married is not a bad idea.

Anyway, Julian is saved from having to respond at all by the arrival of my dressing room-mate, Kris. "Hey, Julian. Hey, Gracie," she greets us as she scoots past Julian in the doorway into the room.

"Hey Kris," we respond simultaneously.

"I'll let you finish changing. I'm sure it's been a long shoot," Julian finally says.

"Indeed, it has," I agree.

"Glad filming is going well and I'm sure we'll run into each other, even if we don't have any scenes together."

"Thanks. I appreciate your stopping by." I feel formal in our conversation, but don't know what, if anything, I could be doing differently. Julian offers a half-wave and then leaves.

When I turn around in the doorway, Kris is watching me speculatively. I choose to ignore the look, but she comments anyway.

"You do know he's married, right?"

"Why does everyone feel the need to remind me of that?" I ask in return. When Kris does not respond, I continue. "Yes, I know that he is married. There is nothing going on between us."

"I don't think you can quite say that," Kris disagrees.

"What do you mean? We haven't done anything."

"I believe that, but I still don't think you can say there is nothing between you. He clearly is interested in you and although you're trying not to be, you're interested in him."

I've been avoiding eye contact with Kris. When she finishes that statement, I turn to look at her. "I agree we have chemistry. That doesn't mean we have to act on it. I have no interest in becoming involved with a coworker at all, let alone one who is married. It just isn't going to happen."

Kris laughs. "I know. I've just never seen him behave this way toward a woman before."

"Really?"

"Even before he was married."

"How long have you known him?"

"Oh, wow, for years. I used to be a regular here and so worked much more closely with Julian. Since I've been dropped back to a recurring character, not as much, but I can honestly say that his behavior is unusual."

"Do you think I should do anything differently?"

"I don't think there's anything you could be doing differently. Based on what I just saw, anyway, I think you're cool. You're being polite and expressing interest in him as a co-worker without suggesting you would be open for something more. Even if both of you might want that."

"That's good to know. I wouldn't want rumors to develop."

"As long as you limit your encounters with Julian to inside of this building, I wouldn't worry about that."

"Anything else…" I begin.

"Would be off limits and not a good idea," Kris continues emphatically.

"I can do that. Thanks for the advice. Besides, I'm only here for three more weeks."

Kris laughs again. "I wouldn't count on a time frame to keep you from temptation. You're fighting some pretty strong chemistry."

I've finished changing and gather my belongings together as I respond. "We're both adults. We can handle a little chemistry."

"Good luck," Kris says. She is changing out of her wardrobe as I leave the room.

I think about my conversation with Julian and Kris' advice and warnings all the way home. This whole situation is crazy. How is it that I've managed to attract the most un-eligible non-bachelor – and he's a coworker. The ringing of my cell phone interrupts my thoughts. I manage to just answer the call before it goes to voice mail.

"Hello?"

"Gracie Corsini, please."

"This is Gracie."

"Gracie, this is Aliana Gregson, from the district attorney's office. Do you have a minute?"

My heart begins beating at a thousand beats per minutes. "Of course," I say, and am amazed at how calm I sound. This is it!

"The grand jury chose to indict Thomas Pullman on all charges." Yes! "He will now have to go to court later this week to submit a plea of guilty or not-guilty to the charges."

"That's wonderful. Congratulations."

"Thank you, but we owe you a great deal for your willingness to go before the grand jury and tell your story. Let me tell you what will happen from here. My office has been communicating with Mr. Pullman's attorney regarding our willingness to make a deal."

"In exchange for him flipping on his boss," I interject.

"Exactly. Thus far, they have been resistant to the idea. Now that the indictments have come down, Mr. Pullman and his attorney may be in a more cooperative mood."

"I certainly hope so."

"As for you, as we discussed, I've arranged for a police officer to provide protection. Here's the catch." Uh-oh. "The plan to secure Mr. Pullman's cooperation is obviously not guaranteed to work. The city does not have the funds to provide protection for any significant length of time. The only reason it was authorized at all is because this is connected to fighting racketeering."

"What does that mean for me?"

"Bottom line. We can provide the protection for at most several weeks. This will hopefully be enough time for Mr. Pullman to recognize that cooperating is in his best interest."

"And if it's not?"

"Then unfortunately, we will have to pull the protection detail and you will be on your own."

"Oh, goody," I can't help but respond with a bit of sarcasm in my voice. "If that's the case, how long until the trial?"

"It would most likely be several months down the road. The wheels of justice turn slowly."

"Is Mr. Pullman or his attorney aware of this time constraint on my protection? I mean, couldn't he and his lawyer, in effect, just string you along until the protection time runs out and then come after me. Would you drop the charges if I wasn't able to testify?" I can feel tendrils of fear spreading along my spine and I shiver involuntarily.

Ms. Gregson sighs softly, but audibly. "No, they are not aware of the specific time constraint. Having said that, Mr. Pullman's attorney is not an idiot and he likely can deduce on his own that your protection wouldn't last long. My office intends to make it clear, however, that we would move forward on the case, with or without your testimony. That should alleviate much of the concern."

"I guess that makes sense," I agree, but I'm not sure how much I'm buying what she's selling. At any rate, the fear isn't dissipating. I mean, this is a guy facing jail time and the state's case seems rather weak without me — at least by my understanding.

"Let's take this one step at a time. Right now, we plan to provide you police protection. I'd like to get that set up as soon as possible. We can deal with the longer-term issues as they arise."

"I guess I don't have much of a choice," I say and Ms. Gregson stays silent. "How does the police protection work?"

"Are you available now?"

"Sure."

"I'll make some phone calls and get everything arranged. If you could head to the police precinct where you originally made your report, I'll have your bodyguard waiting. He can explain how this kind of detail works. How does that sound?"

"That sounds good. I'll head over there now."

"Good. I'll talk to you later." The connection ceases. Why hadn't I thought out all of the possibilities? It seemed highly likely to me that Tommy would simply bide his time until my protection was pulled and then — wham — he could take me out… or whatever gangsta phrase is appropriate. I sigh. Oh well, just one more chapter in my ongoing soap opera life.

As I make the now familiar walk to the police station, the action finally does dissipate the fear and I consider all of the implications of what Ms. Gregson told me on the telephone. Really, this whole business has become much more complicated than it needed to be. Why couldn't Tommy have conducted his drug sale in another dark alley? This rather unproductive line of thinking stops when I find myself once again outside the police station. Unlike before, I enter the station with confidence and stride purposefully over to the desk sergeant.

"Hello. My name is Graciella Corsini. Assistant district attorney Aliana Gregson should have called about me?" I state this last as more of a question. The sergeant consults a sheaf of papers before answering.

"Yep, here you are. If you'll have a seat," he says, indicating some wooden benches I had missed on my earlier visit to the station, "the officer will be with you shortly."

"Thank you very much." I turn and head toward the benches. Sitting down, I note that these are not the most comfortable benches in the world. Thankfully, I don't have to sit on them long before a young man in jeans and a long-sleeved tee shirt approaches.

"Graciella Corsini?" The young man appears to be in his mid-twenties with highly chiseled features, and the body under his shirt clearly indicates a significant amount of time spent at the gym. But, he doesn't look like an over-developed gym rat. His curly blond hair seems in need of a haircut and, when he smiles, his slightly skewed lower teeth lend him a boyish innocence.

"Yes?" Is this my bodyguard? Or my bodyguard's assistant?

"I'm Officer Robert Sanders."

"Hello, Officer Sanders."

"Please, call me Bobby. After all, we'll be working rather closely together for awhile."

"You're my police protection, Bobby?"

"The day person, anyway."

I furrow my brow in confusion. "Day person?"

Bobby glances around the waiting area. "Why don't you come on back and I can explain how all of this is going to work?"

"That would be fantastic." I rise from the bench and follow Bobby as he heads to the back offices. To my surprise, rather than go to his office (or more likely, cubicle), Bobby leads us to what appears to be a break room.

"I thought this would be more comfortable than sitting in the noisy squad room." We sit in plastic seats at what I swear is a plastic table. Guess they have to save the money for expenses like protective service somewhere.

"Who'd have thought a break room would be quieter than the office area?" I ask this with a smile.

"No kidding. Anyway, as I started to say out front, I'm the day shift person. Basically, there are two approximately twelve-hour shifts and I have the day shift. One of my colleagues will take the night shift. And, actually, that person will likely change every couple of days. I, on the other hand, will remain the day shift person the entire time you have police protection."

"Am I going to have a bunch of random police officers in my apartment?" I feel like maybe I missed something.

"No, sorry. I probably should have explained how that worked first. When you enter a building, I will go in ahead of you, just to check things out. When I'm comfortable that there's nothing to be concerned about, I will take up a post outside the building and keep watch until I see you exit."

"You'll be monitoring the perimeter?" It seems like I've heard that phrase before on television.

Bobby smiles. "More or less."

"You'll then walk with me anywhere I go until the end of the day, when someone else takes over."

"Exactly. Whenever you're in for the night, I'll head home to get some sleep and another officer will set up outside your apartment to make sure things are okay."

"Does that mean I'll have to be in by a certain time? I'm an actress and sometimes filming can run pretty late," I explain, for some reason not wanting him to think it's my party animal ways that could be a problem.

"We expect that your schedule may sometimes be erratic. That's why I said approximately twelve-hour shifts. If I need to stay on a little longer, that's okay."

"While I am certainly appreciative of all of this, I can't imagine this is a plum assignment for you." I am starting to feel bad about how boring this must seem to him.

Bobby smiles again. "Don't even worry about it. I don't mind assignments like this now and then. Especially when I get to protect such a lovely woman."

"Thanks," I respond with a smile. "By the way, how long have you been a cop?"

"Three years and, before you ask, I love it."

I laugh. This might actually be fun, having a personal bodyguard. "I suppose we should get going. I don't have much planned for the remainder of the day, but I'd like to introduce you to my roommate, Jane."

"Let's roll, then," Bobby says and we stand up in unison. We detour through the cubicles so that he can grab his jacket to go over his shoulder-holster and gun. Then, we wind our way back through to the front lobby and out into the beginning dusk. I note with interest how Bobby scans the crowds as we walk, apparently constantly aware of our surroundings, though I suspect the average person wouldn't even notice what he is doing.

"This is my apartment building," I announce needlessly, as we come to a halt outside the front door. True to his word, after scanning briefly behind us, Bobby enters the building before I do. His quick check of the lobby area does not turn up any bad guys intent on any dastardly deeds. Bobby beckons me in and I walk past him to check the mail. After collecting the meager items (mostly bills, blech), we head toward the elevator. We're silent on the ride to my floor and Bobby exits the elevator before I do, but the hallway is so small that this only delays me about a nanosecond. We can hear a voice coming through my apartment door as we approach. I note that Jane does not sound happy, although I cannot understand specific words through the door.

"That noise you hear would be my roommate, Jane," I explain as I unlock (hey, this is New York) and open the door. Jane barely acknowledges our presence.

"How many times am I going to have to explain this? My statement never arrived, so I was unaware that my due date changed. Since it was not my fault, I want the late fee and finance charges removed from my total." Jane listens to the individual on the other end of the line. "I understand that's the general policy. But, you changed my due date without notifying me first, so this is as much your fault as it is mine or the post office."

"They better just agree with her and remove the charges," I whisper to Bobby as we walk to the couch and have a seat. "She'll never let this go."

"I'd like to speak to a supervisor, please," Jane finally says, without sounding overly irritated. While she's on hold waiting, she turns to us. "Hey, Gracie and new guy. Give me a minute and this will all be taken care of." She switches focus back to the phone. "Hello, Sharon. Thank you for assisting me with this."

"Hey, let me give you a quick tour of the apartment while she's on the phone," I say to Bobby in another stage whisper.

"Okay," he whispers back as we rise and head toward the bedroom. We can hear Jane as she discusses the issue with the supervisor.

"As I tried to explain to the customer service representative, I understand that it's my responsibility if I make a late payment due to not receiving my statement on time, or at all. However, I still would have been on time if the due date hadn't been changed – if I had known about the change."

"This is my bedroom." I gesture into the room and then we walk past.

"As you can see on my account, I paid online two days before the payment normally would have been due. When I realized my statement had gotten lost or something, I popped on the computer to pay it anyway. Imagine my surprise when I see that I was already late because of the date change." Jane listens to Sharon the customer service representative supervisor say supervisor-type things.

Whatever she's saying, I can see from Jane's visible relaxing that it's in her favor. "Thank you very much for handling this matter." Jane hangs up the phone and turns to us with a sigh.

"This is the bathroom," I gesture to the tiny room. Bobby and I continue to make the circuit of the apartment.

Jane joins us, explaining the call we walked in on. "You wouldn't think that issue would be so difficult to understand. You can't expect me to know about a change I've never been notified about. Right?"

"Absolutely," I immediately agree. "At least it sounds like it worked out well." I turn my attention to Bobby. "This is Jane's bedroom and that's obviously the kitchen."

"Yeah, once I got past the duck who answered the phone." Tour complete, Bobby and I return to sit on the couch.

By the way, the 'duck' comment will only make sense if you're aware of the 'ducks and eagles' inspirational speech that Pat Riley used to give when he gave those speeches. My brother heard it once, years ago, and told it to me. If you don't know it, look it up online. You'll love it.

"Oh, hey, let me introduce you to Officer Robert Sanders," I say, realizing that I haven't introduced the two of them because Jane was handling her business. "He's my police protection."

"That means Tommy was indicted," Jane states her question.

"Yep. Bobby will be hanging out with me for a couple of weeks."

"It's nice to meet you, Bobby," Jane says, coming over to offer him her hand.

"You, as well, Jane," Bobby replies as they shake hands.

"Are you going to be staying in the apartment?" Jane clearly wants to know this because we don't exactly have a ton of room for an additional person.

"Not at all," Bobby laughs and explains the situation to Jane. After completing that explanation, he turns to me. "By the way, one thing I didn't mention is that it's your choice, when we're out, how obvious or not you want me to be about the protection."

"You mean, announcing your presence or wearing shades or something," I joke.

"Sort of. I can make it very clear to people that I am a bodyguard of some kind or I can be fairly subtle."

"Which would you recommend?" Jane asks this question.

"I'd go with subtlety because being obvious will clearly draw attention to you and, honestly, we don't want to draw a lot of attention."

"What about the idea of making it clear to Tommy or any of his thugs that I'm under police protection?" I ask this out of curiosity more than because I advocate this position.

"That is why some officers prefer to be more in your face than I do. I happen to feel that extra attention is never a good thing. Besides, it's likely that any associates of Tommy would recognize I'm a police officer anyway. Your more competent criminals seem to have a sixth sense about that."

"You've convinced me," I declare. "Let's go with subtlety."

"I have a couple of quick questions and then I'll leave you two to your evening."

"Fire away."

"I didn't notice one, but I want to make sure there are no other entrances to the apartment besides the front door."

"The apartment isn't big enough to have more than one entrance," Jane comments with a laugh.

"Do all of the windows have locks on them?"

Jane and I look at each other while we think about that. "Yes," I finally say. "They definitely do. In fact, I remember my father double checking that when we moved in because he wanted to make sure I'd be safe."

"Good. Make sure you keep the windows shut and locked at all times. Since it's still fairly cool out, I don't imagine that will be a problem."

"Not at all," I say.

"In that case, I'll leave now." Bobby glances at his watch. "It's almost six. Do you have plans to go out to dinner or anything?"

"No, I'm worn out from the day."

"Okay. I'll call the night shift person to take over and I will see you in the morning." We synchronize our watches for the morning and then Bobby leaves.

"He seems nice and competent," Jane comments after Bobby has left.

"I think so, too," I agree.

"Can you believe those people at the credit card company?" Jane switches topics. "How am I supposed to know the date was changed? Sheesh. It's unfortunate that this is the month my statement seems to have gotten lost in the mail."

"No kidding," I say, but there is an idea gnawing its way to consciousness. "At least it got taken care of."

"True," Jane says. "What?" She notices a look on my face, apparently.

"What?" I respond back with this because what has just bubbled to the surface is a memory of the day our mailbox was open. Could someone have really stolen our mail?

"You have a look on your face."

"I always have some kind of look," I say dismissively.

"Should I be worried about the police protection?" Jane switches topics again.

"Well, no, that's the point of having the protection," I answer with a smile.

"I know that, smart ass. You know what I mean."

"According to the assistant district attorney, we'll have Bobby for a few weeks while they try to get Tommy to roll over on his boss."

"And if he doesn't."

"If he doesn't," I hesitate, "eventually I won't have the protection."

"Even though he'll still be out there, knowing you're testifying against him."

"I know it's not the ideal situation, but why don't we wait and see what happens in the next couple of weeks." Listen to me, the voice of reason and calm. That's a switch.

"I'll try. You know me, I have a tendency to worry."

"You? No, of course not," I comment with a touch of good-natured sarcasm. Jane smiles and rolls her eyes at me.

CHAPTER SEVENTEEN

"People have to go through security, including a metal detector, to get past the lobby," I explain to Bobby after we reach the studio. We are standing outside the door, beginning to argue.

"I told you, part of my job is to check out where you'll be to make sure that the area is safe and secure. Then, I can leave and watch the outside," he explains again.

"Even though there's a security guard and everything?"

"Even though. Listen, I get that you aren't thrilled about having me where you work, but this is part of the safety package we offer. I can't say I'm doing everything I can if you prevent me from doing everything I was trained to do."

I feel myself relenting. "You'll just go in, check the rooms, and then wait out here for me?"

"That's it," he assures me. "Nothing to it."

"Okay, let's go," I consent and open the studio door. Bobby steps past me to enter first and heads to the security guard, who has risen to greet us.

"I'm Officer Robert Sanders," he begins, reaching for his badge. "I've been assigned to protect Ms. Corsini." George, the security guard, analyzes the badge and, apparently satisfied, allows him to pass through the area without going through the metal detector. I, on the other hand, still have to do those things. After I am inspected and also pass muster, I lead Bobby through the maze of hallways to my dressing room.

Of course when I was hoping this would be a quick in and out inspection, all three of my dressing room-mates are present.

"Danielle, Megan, Kris, this is Bobby. He's…um…checking things out. He won't be staying," I say weakly. The three women greet him in a friendly, but slightly disinterested manner, as they are focused on preparing for their upcoming scenes. This is actually a good thing, because I hopefully won't have to explain the long ridiculous story of my police escort.

"Everything looks fine, Gracie," Bobby says quietly. "I'll wait for you outside. Give me a call when you're finished filming, okay?"

"Will do," I reply, with a saucy salute. As I do, I notice Julian has arrived in our doorway. Oh, this should be fun…well, interesting, anyway.

"Good morning, Julian. How was your weekend?"

"It was fine, Gracie. How was yours?" Our formal exchange is not lost on Bobby, and Julian's presence has even pulled the women's attention.

"It was fine." Julian stares back and forth between Bobby and me. With a sigh, I continue, "Julian, this is Bobby. Bobby, this is Julian." The two men shake hands and I can see them visually sizing each other up. Good grief.

I can see the question on Julian's face, but he simply says he'll see us later and departs.

"He likes you," Bobby says with certainty.

Kris makes a noise of assent and the other two women act as though they've suddenly become deaf and blind and missed the entire exchange.

"He's married," I respond as if this negates his statement. Bobby smiles at me, but drops the subject.

"Call me," he repeats and then leaves.

I wait for one of the women to say something as I change into my wardrobe for the first scene, and they do not disappoint.

"I told you," Kris says in a knowing tone.

"There's nothing going on between us," I try again in vain to assert.

"He never visited this room before you arrived," Megan chimes in.

"That's true," Danielle agrees.

"Listen, seriously, I obviously can't say what's in his mind, but I do not get involved with married men. I can't stress this enough. Please, please let this go," I find myself pleading with them.

"Relax, Gracie," Kris says. "We're just teasing you."

I am saved from any more commentary from the peanut gallery by the presence of the icy blond from my first day.

"Five minutes," she imparts her wisdom and then begins to depart the room.

"Hey," I stop her, suddenly inspired. Maybe if I'm nice to her, she'll thaw out. I just don't like it when people don't seem to like me – especially when I haven't done anything to them. "Thanks," I say with a smile. The blond looks impassively at me, then turns and leaves. I don't know what to make of that, but am glad that the others in the room missed the exchange.

I'm not actually in the first scene of the day, but Kris and Megan are, so they head for the set.

"Neither of you may plan to do anything, but the rumors are already flying about his obvious interest in you," Danielle says quickly, as though our conversation had not been interrupted by the presence of the blond P.A. or the departure of Kris and Megan.

"Really?"

"A few of the guys even have bets going on how long it will take for the two of you to sleep together."

"Oh, that's just great." I love being the subject of gossip.

"You know what?"

"What?"

"I wouldn't worry about it at all. If you truly don't plan to have an affair with him, and I think you've made it pretty clear that you don't, then do whatever you want."

"Thanks."

Danielle smiles encouragingly at me and then exits the room. I briefly sit there with my thoughts before deciding to head to hair and makeup.

The rest of the day on set goes by in a blur and then I'm back in the dressing room changing when someone knocks on the door. I pull my shirt on over my head and call out, "Come in."

The door slowly pushes in and Julian's head peeks around hesitantly.

"C'mon in," I say with a smile. "I don't bite."

Julian smiles less hesitantly and enters the room. He leaves the door open (so no wild imaginations can be triggered, no doubt) and sits in Megan's chair.

"Can we talk?" Oh, no, that's never good.

"Sure."

"I feel like things are awkward between us and I don't understand why," he starts.

"You don't understand why," I echo.

"No, I don't."

He looks so confused that I try for complete honesty.

"Well, the whole cast and crew can tell we're attracted to each other and you're married. I think that sums it up."

"We haven't done anything," he protests, sounding like me earlier.

"I know that, and so do they, actually, but that's not the point."

"It isn't?"

"Generally when a man and a woman are attracted to each other, the more time they spend together, the more likely they are to…" I trail off.

"You don't believe a man and a woman can be friends?"

"Of course I do. It can just be much more difficult if there's an attraction, especially mutual attraction, thrown into the mix."

"I admit I'm attracted to you, but I'd also like a chance to get to know you. I'd like us to try to be friends."

"Do you believe you can just be friends with me?"

"Yes."

Yeah, right. "Okay, then. Let's have lunch."

"Yeah?"

"We can try. You can never have too many friends," I say with a laugh.

"Definitely," Julian agrees. "What about a late lunch right now?"

"You don't have any more filming today?"

"Nope. What do you say?"

"Let's do it. Give me a few minutes to change into my jeans and we'll head out."

Julian agrees and closes the door behind him to allow me to change. I call Bobby to let him know I'm finished and that we're getting lunch.

Bobby's eyebrows rise in a knowing arch when I exit the building with Julian, and I choose to ignore the unspoken comment. He and Julian nod at each other as we meet up.

"We've decided to have lunch in the park," I say brightly. "We're going to grab sandwiches at a deli around the corner Julian knows and then walk over there. Maybe have lunch by the fountain?" I ask Julian.

"That sounds good to me," Julian agrees.

"Is that okay?" I ask Bobby, uncertain about the safety implications of being in such a wide-open space.

"It's not ideal, of course, but we can make it happen," Bobby responds.

"Great," I enthuse and we begin walking toward the sandwich shop. Julian looks as though he wants to say something, probably ask why I checked with Bobby, but stays silent. "I know that must seem weird, but, um, it's complicated. I'll explain later," I answer his unasked question. He stares for a second at Bobby before smiling at me.

"No worries, Gracie."

Julian and I chatter mindlessly while Bobby stays alert a step or so behind us. I think I'm going to like this "just friends" relationship with Julian. If I just think of him like one of my gay male friends, then I can't think of him as having any romantic potential. Despite still finding him wildly attractive…

After collecting our sandwiches, we walk to the fountain I had been thinking of and sit on a low concrete bench. Bobby takes up sentry some distance away.

"This looks great," I say, as I unwrap my mozzarella and tomato with basil panini.

"Mm-mm," Julian agrees, having already taken a bite of his. "It is. You can't go wrong with tomato and mozzarella."

"Definitely not." I take a bite and a soft moan of pleasure escapes when the flavors mingle in my mouth.

"Especially being a vegetarian, it's an option almost always available at delis and such," Julian comments, before taking another large bite.

"You're a vegetarian?" I ask this, almost not wanting him to confirm what he just said.

"Yep. I guess you didn't know that."

"No, I didn't. I'm a vegetarian, too," I tell him.

He's talented, attractive, nice…and he's a vegetarian. This is such torment.

Julian looks surprised. "Oh, I didn't know that. Although, I don't know why I should be surprised. I could sense your gentle soul when we first met."

I laugh at that. "My gentle soul?"

He colors slightly at my response. "Never mind."

Now I feel embarrassed. "I'm sorry. You were complimenting me and I react by poking fun. Thank you for the compliment. I like to believe I'm a nice person, I just never thought about having a gentle soul."

"Well, you're welcome."

Julian and I are silent for a few minutes while we eat our sandwiches in earnest. I close my eyes while I chew my last bite and tilt my face toward the sky, feeling the warmth of the sun. When I open my eyes again, I find Julian staring at me. He quickly averts his gaze. I choose not to comment. We're just friends, right?

"It is such a beautiful day. You know what would be fun today?"

"What?"

"To go sailing. Can you imagine sitting on a boat tooling around the harbor, or the bay, or wherever?" I can practically smell the salt as I imagine the scene I'm setting.

"That sounds wonderful. Too bad we don't have a boat. Besides, I don't know how to sail," Julian admits.

"Neither do I," I say. "You know what we do have, though."

"What?"

"Paddleboats."

"Perfect," Julian agrees enthusiastically.

"Really? Most people think they're childish."

"Not at all. Plus, they don't require any skills whatsoever."

"Exactly."

"And I have an idea to get us ready to head out on the water."

"Yeah?"

Julian stands up, reaches over to take my balled up sandwich wrapper. I follow him as he walks to the nearest garbage receptacle. I notice Bobby has reacted to our movement and is prepared to follow my lead.

"Hop on my back."

"What?" I laugh, uncertain if he is serious.

"Hop on my back," Julian repeats.

"Why?"

"Just do it, Gracie."

"Fine," I say with a smile and jump on Julian's back. He is now carrying me piggyback style, something I haven't done since I was a kid.

"Ready?"

"I guess so." As soon as he begins moving, I know where he's headed. "Wait," I try to intervene but it is too late.

Julian takes us straight into the path of the water spouting out of the fountain. I involuntarily shriek as the first cold droplets of water begin to fall on us. Julian runs in and out of the fountain's path, so to speak, such that we never get drenched, but only slightly damp. After several minutes of this, he moves completely out of the span of the falling water and I slide off of his back.

"Are you ready to go paddle boating now?"

"Yes," I say, laughing. "But, explain to me how getting wet prepares us for going on the boat. It's not like paddleboats create monstrous waves or anything."

"That's true. I guess it doesn't really prepare us for anything. It just seemed like a good idea."

I laugh at his 'explanation' and we begin making our way toward the paddleboat rental area. I see in my peripheral vision that Bobby is following, a discreet distance behind.

After Julian pays a rather exorbitant amount of money to ride on a paddleboat, he and I paddle fervently away from the shore. There's a companionable silence as we concentrate on paddling. When we are more or less in the middle of the lake, Julian slows and then stops the motion of his legs.

"Have we arrived?" I ask with a smile.

"Can I ask you something?" Uh-oh.

"Sure."

"Who is Bobby? I'm not an idiot. He seems to be protecting you, but you're really not famous," Julian says this last in an attempt at levity.

"What do you mean, I'm not famous??" I ask in mock surprise.

"Well, you're not quite famous," he responds with a smile.

I laugh. "Yeah, he's protecting me. Don't worry, though. You're probably not in any danger," I quip.

"I'm not worried about me. I'm wondering if I should be worried about you."

"Let me tell you a little story," I begin and then explain the entire lovely situation to him.

"That doesn't seem like a good resolution to me," Julian asserts when I finish. "You have a bodyguard for an indeterminate, but probably short, amount of time, while this asshole may or may not decide to flip on his boss. And, if any of that doesn't work out, well, too bad for Gracie."

"You seem more upset about this than I am," I comment.

"Well, I, um," Julian seems uncertain what to say and this uncertainty calms him down. "I just don't want you to get hurt."

"Neither do I, and neither does Bobby. That's why he's here."

"I suppose so."

"Do you think I should have just ignored the whole thing and not gotten involved?"

"Of course not."

"Then accept what it is and let's move on," I say, touching his arm lightly. "It'll all work out. Things usually do."

Julian flashes his brilliant smile. "You are absolutely right. Let's talk about something else." And so we engage in getting-to-know-you chitchat as we lazily meander around the lake.

I haven't wanted to say anything, but the devil in my brain forces my mouth to speak. "This is probably none of my business, but is your wife really pregnant?"

I regret the question the instant the words leave my lips as I see his mouth tighten into an unhappy line.

"You know what? Never mind. Forget I even asked," I quickly try to backpedal. "It's none of my business."

Julian sighs. "No, it's okay. Friends talk about their personal lives, right?" He offers me a tired smile. I nod, but say nothing. "To answer your question. No, she isn't pregnant. Was she ever pregnant? I don't know. She insists that she was and miscarried the baby. I don't know what to believe."

Since I've already gone and made an ass out of myself, I continue with my inappropriate personal questions. "Would you have married her if you hadn't thought she was pregnant?"

Julian pauses so long I think he isn't going to answer the question, and then he does. "No, probably not," he says quietly.

"Will you stay with her?" I can't believe I'm asking him these questions, but I feel like I need to know them somehow.

"I don't know." He stares morosely out across the water. I lean over my side of the boat and use my hands to splash as much water on him as I can.

"What the-?" He looks startled, but the morose look disappears.

"I just thought you maybe were feeling too dry. I was helping," I tell him with my most innocent expression.

"Then allow me to help as well."

Julian leans over his side of the boat and begins splashing me back. It's somewhat physically awkward, leaning over the side of the boat like that, but we laugh as we splash each other like children.

"Enough," I finally say. "I'm soaked."

"You started it."

"That's mature."

"Who lied and said I was mature?"

We smile at each other and warning bells begin going off in my mind. You are veering out of the friends' zone. Danger, Gracie Corsini, danger.

"As much fun as this has been," I begin and glance at my watch. "It's getting late and I should probably be getting home."

"If you must."

"Yes, I must. Thank you for a wonderful time."

"You're welcome. Thanks for the great paddleboat suggestion."

We have been paddling back to shore while speaking and soon find ourselves back on dry land. I notice Bobby nearby watching me and the surrounding people.

"I see your bodyguard seems ready to go," Julian comments.

"Yeah. He probably didn't much like the open spaces of this entire afternoon. But, I did." I say this last and then am flooded with uncertainty. If this were a date, this would be when we would lock lips. Since we're just friends, I am at a loss as to the proper protocol. Julian seems to be equally flummoxed.

"Well, then. I guess this is goodbye. I'm not filming again until next week, so I'll see you then."

"Okay, I'll see you then. Enjoy your time off." We exchange an awkward quick hug.

As Julian walks away, I realize the thought that I won't see him again until the following week saddens me. I mentally shake myself. Get a grip. This is ridiculous. You don't feel this way about any of your other friends, I remind myself. Yeah, and there's a reason for that. I tell my inner self to shut up and turn my attention to Bobby, who is walking up to me.

"Are you ready to go?"

"Yes," I reply, without much enthusiasm.

"What's the matter? I thought you had a good time today?"

"That's what's the matter."

"Ohh," he says knowingly and falls silent.

CHAPTER EIGHTEEN

"Jane, we're so glad you came," my mother gushes to my roommate. Apparently I'm chopped liver. Oh well. If it makes my mother happy. Of course, little does my mother know that the real reason Jane came with me to family dinner is not because she's been invited about a zillion times but because she didn't want to stay in the apartment alone. Eh, but whatever the reason, her presence makes my mother happy. They head off to the kitchen and I hear the words *recipe* and *chef* float out of the air. Then Bobby steps into view behind me and the activity in the house ceases. Even my mother senses the change and turns from her conversation with Jane.

"Everyone, this is Bobby. He's a friend of mine. Not a boyfriend," I quickly clarify, so that there will be absolutely no confusion on the subject. With my family, subtlety is a lost art form. My brother is the closest so he introduces himself first.

"Hey, Bobby, I'm Anthony, Gracie's older brother." The two men shake hands.

"I'm Maria," my sister calls from the couch, without bothering to get up. She does at least wave. She looks pissed and

I wonder how the conversation had been going before we arrived.

My father had risen when he first saw Bobby and now approaches. "I'm Tomas, Graciella's father. She has never mentioned you before," he says with a pointed look toward me.

"Do not be rude to our guest," my mother admonishes my father, as she hurries over to give Bobby a hug. "I'm Annabella, Graciella's mother."

"It's nice to meet all of you," Bobby replies, appearing slightly overwhelmed by the shaking and hugging. I suppose I could have warned him, but this is much more fun.

"Everyone quit crowding in the doorway and have a seat in the living room," my mother encourages, as she and Jane continue toward the kitchen. I've established that Bobby is not a potential husband, so my mother is more interested in talking cooking with Jane.

After we all have taken seats, my father and sister resume the discussion (well, argument) they had been having before we arrived.

"I'm tired of having this discussion," my sister grumbles.

"Then quit bringing it up," my father suggests. Maria gives him a watered down version of our mother's evil eye.

"It's my life," she continues anyway.

"And you can do whatever you want — after you finish college," my father says with finality and turns away from Maria. She actually crosses her arms in front of her chest. I can't believe she's sulking. What is she, nine? "So, Bobby, how do you know Graciella?"

I sigh and decide to just tell them the truth. "I've had a busy few weeks since I was last here," I begin. "Bobby is a police officer. He's my bodyguard." I pause at the expected peppering of questions.

"He's what?" Maria asks.

"What do you need a bodyguard for?" My father immediately questions.

"Did I hear the word bodyguard?" My mother calls this from the kitchen before appearing in the doorway.

"Police officer?" This final question is from my brother.

"Are you all finished?" They remain silent. "Good. Then I can continue." I quickly tell them the story of Average Guy and the drug deal, the vague (and not-so-vague) threats on my life, and the district attorney's recommendation that I have a bodyguard in the interim.

"If I'm understanding you correctly, this is a very temporary situation," my brother states.

"Yes," I assure the family. Did I forget to mention the high likelihood that Tommy won't flip on his boss and I'll be without protection for months? Oops, my bad. What my family doesn't know keeps my mother from having a coronary.

The family asks a few more questions and then miraculously drops the subject. My mother and Jane decide to join us and squeeze in on the available furniture.

"How's the soap opera going?" My sister asks this question, in part out of curiosity, but also in part to remind my father than I have a job unrelated to my college degree.

"It's going great," I answer enthusiastically. "It's only been two weeks, but I feel like they're my second family. Everyone has been so nice and welcoming."

"A certain someone in particular," Jane says in a singsong voice.

"What? What is she talking about?" My mother, who has radar for these sorts of things, senses a man in this story.

"Thanks, Jane."

"No problem." She smiles sweetly in my direction and I roll my eyes.

"There's this guy," I begin.

"Is he hot?" My sister can always be counted on for the important angles.

"Is he single?" My mother wants me to get married and give her grandbabies.

"Is he an actor or does he have a real job?" My father has never been too fond of my acting. It's not a "real" job.

My brother stays silent and when I look in his direction to see if he has anything to add, he simply shakes his head and chuckles softly.

"To answer your questions, yes, Julian is hot, and yes, he is an actor, which is a real job, papa. And, no, mama, he's not single." My mother looks crestfallen.

"For the moment," Jane chimes in again.

"Seriously, Jane. Could you try not to help so much?" If looks could kill she'd be…seriously maimed. She smiles again.

"What does Jane mean? Are you having an affair with a married man?" My mother looks to heaven as though God can help her with her wayward child.

"No, I am not having an affair. We're just friends. He *is* in an unhappy marriage, but I have made it clear that we would only be friends," I clarify for the family.

"An unhappy marriage?" My mother asks this and I notice she now has a look of consideration on her face.

"Yeah, apparently. You may have seen something about it on one of the entertainment shows."

"Wait a minute," my sister says and sits up abruptly. "You don't mean Julian McNamara, do you?"

"Um, yes, I do."

"Oh wow, he is definitely a hottie. And, yeah, he does seem to be in an unhappy marriage. Don't worry, mama, if anyone is worth leaving his wife for, it's Gracie."

My mother looks horrified by my sister's comment. Marriage is sacrosanct in this household.

"Okay, sorry," Maria says sheepishly. "That didn't come out exactly right."

I have had enough of this conversation. "Okay, that's my life right now. What about you, Anthony? How are things at the station? Have you met anyone?" Thankfully, the family's focus swivels to Anthony, who still manages to shoot me a look before answering their questions.

The rest of the evening goes quite smoothly. Jane and my mother exchange several recipes, the food tastes delicious (of course, it always does), and my father and sister did not resume their argument. All in all, a successful family dinner. We stay later than I planned, but it is worth it. I relax the rest of the weekend and am raring to go Monday morning when I'm due back at the studio.

Who knew how much that rest and relaxation would come in handy in the next few weeks?

CHAPTER NINETEEN

"Good morning, Gracie," Bobby greets me the moment I step outside my apartment building.

"Morning, Bobby."

"Steve tells me it was another quiet night."

"Yep, nobody tried to kill me. That's always a good thing."

"Is anything wrong?"

"Why? What makes you ask?" Like I don't know. Maybe it's my bitchy tone this morning. I actually don't know what's wrong with me.

"You just seem a little… tense."

"I'm just tired. Or maybe I woke up on the wrong side of the bed," I offer as my non-explanation.

"Okay, if you say so." Bobby looks like he wants to say something else, reconsiders it, and remains silent. Our walk to the studio is uncharacteristically quiet as I wallow in my unusual state of malaise.

"Morning, George," Bobby greets the security guard after we've entered the studio building. "All quiet?"

"No problems here, officer."

"Great." Bobby turns to me. "Have a good day shooting and I'll see you when you're finished."

"Sounds good." I smile brightly as a wordless apology for earlier and head toward the dressing room. I continue to muse about my attitude. I realize as I approach my dressing room that I am feeling perkier, more like my normal self.

What does this mean? Maybe I'm tired of having a bodyguard? Although, I definitely like the added layer of protection having Bobby affords me. My arrival at the dressing room saves me from further musings. Danielle is the only one of my mates already present. She's brushing her flaming red hair as she seems to be critically eyeing her wardrobe for her first scene of the day.

"Do you think the purple in this shirt clashes with my hair color?"

"What?" I focus fully on her and the color concern. "No, not at all. Actually, I think the purple makes the red in your hair stand out even more."

"It doesn't stand out too much?"

"Not at all," I assure her. "I think it looks great."

"Hi, Gracie," comes a voice from the door. I notice my heart does a little flip-flop.

Oh, God, that's not good.

"Good morning, Julian," I respond before even turning. "I didn't think you were filming this week."

"They added some scenes," he explains before asking, "How was your weekend?"

"Great. I did family dinner on Saturday. That's always fun. Or at least interesting," I amend.

"Your family's in the area?" Danielle joins the conversation with this question.

"Yeah, my mother, father, and brother live in Brooklyn. My sister lives in Manhattan."

"That's nice. My family lives in Minnesota and I only get to see them about twice a year. What about you, Julian? You never talk about your family."

"Most of my family lives in southern California. I see them on major holidays and if I'm out there filming." Julian seems a bit baffled about how this conversation came about. He turns back to me. "Anyway, Gracie, before I head over to hair and makeup, I wanted to see if you wanted to get lunch tomorrow. I have an early day and I noticed you do, too."

I can see Danielle's look in the mirror and hope Julian missed it. "That sounds great. We'll figure out the details tomorrow."

"Talk to you then."

"Interesting," Danielle begins after he leaves.

"It's just lunch."

"It's still interesting."

"We're just friends."

"I didn't say you weren't."

I sigh and choose to opt out of the conversation. A few minutes later, while I'm changing my clothing, Danielle heads toward the door.

"Very interesting," she says with a smile before ducking out, as I sail a balled up sock in her direction.

"We're just friends," I mutter to my reflection. So what if my mood instantly improved when he arrived. So what if my heart goes pitter-pat when he's near. Good lord, I sound like an 80s rock ballad.

CHAPTER TWENTY

"How was filming today?"

"It went well, Bobby," I respond as he joins me outside the studio door.

"And your boyfriend?"

"Very funny," I tell him as I give him a slight shove. He smiles.

"You mean he's not your boyfriend?"

"You know damn well he's not," I retort tartly.

"When are you seeing him next?"

"Lunch tomorrow," I answer without thinking.

"Hmm-mmm."

"You know, friends have lunch, too."

"I didn't say anything."

"Your noise said it all." Sheesh, why couldn't people give it a rest?

"Sorry, sorry, I'll stop."

"Thanks."

We move on to more mundane topics as we continue the trek to my apartment. I see a familiar figure as we near the entrance to my building and groan inwardly. My family members never make the journey down here. This can't be good.

"Hey, papa," I call out and he turns in surprise.

"Oh, good, you are home, Graciella."

"Well, almost," I correct him with a smile. He doesn't return the smile. "Who died?"

"Your sister dropped out of NYU," he says without preamble and my hearts sinks. I can't believe she actually did it.

"What happened?" I open the door to the building, wait for Bobby to do his check, and then wave to him as he silently moves off to wherever he goes to protect me; my father follows me inside.

"Does it matter? She dropped out. You have to talk some sense into her."

"Now wait just a minute. I don't want to get in the middle of this. It's Maria's choice whether or not to stay in school."

"Bullshit," my father says angrily and my eyebrows just about shoot off of my forehead. My father never curses. It would offend a saint or something…oh, wait, he's still talking.

"-and tell her to go back," he finishes, as I open the door to my apartment. Jane's mouth opens in surprise when she sees our guest.

"Papa, I can't tell her to go back. It's her life. If she wants to leave, there truly isn't anything you can do. What made her leave now? She's been talking about this forever," I ask, genuinely curious what on Earth could have happened for her to actually drop out.

"I don't know. She said something about a contract. It doesn't matter. Education is the most important thing. She must go back." He glares at me stubbornly. I sigh, knowing this will never end if I don't capitulate.

"If I promise to talk to her, will you relax?"

"Yes. Tell her to go back."

"I'll talk to her, but I'm not making any promises," I warn him, although I am fairly certain this will fall on deaf ears.

"Yes, you will talk to her. She will return to school. It will be alright." My father is nodding to himself. Yep, deaf ears.

"Okay, okay, papa. I'll talk to her. Do you want to stay for dinner, since you came all the way down here?"

"No, your mother's cooking is better."

"Thanks," I say with a laugh, since this is absolutely the truth. "You could have called."

"Not as pushy to make a call," my father says with a sly smile as he heads for the door.

"I'll remember that," I respond and give him a quick hug as he leaves.

I shut the door behind him with another sigh.

"What are you going to do?"

"Jane, I have no idea. I guess I'll have to drag her ass out to talk to me."

*****

"Okay, Maria, spill," I order my sister before she can even sit. I called and invited her out to dinner probably before my father even reached the exit to my apartment building. Sensing the inevitability of my harassing her, she agreed.

"Was it mama or papa?"

"Papa. And he came in person," I emphasize.

"No way. He never comes into Manhattan," Maria says, eyes widening in shock.

"And he cursed. That's how big of a tragedy this apparently is," I explain, as though this needs any explanation. "Tell me about this contract papa mentioned."

"I've been offered a contract with one of the biggest cosmetics companies in the world."

"Really?"

"Yes! I'm going to be in all of their advertising."

"Holy cow!"

"Print and television," she says with obvious excitement. "It's so cool. And, the money is spectacular."

"I can only imagine. I certainly understand why you dropped out. Shoot, I probably would have, too, if I have been given that opportunity."

Maria's eyes well up.

"Hey, why are you crying?"

"Thank you."

"For what? I haven't done anything."

"For understanding. You'll help, right?"

"You're most certainly welcome. Help with what?" I ask this, already knowing the answer.

"You can explain to mama and papa why this is a good thing and they'll be okay with it," she says with enthusiasm, already imagining the issue blowing over because of my divine intervention. Oh, boy.

"I'll talk to them, but I can't guarantee anything will come of it," I tell her, expecting this warning to go over about as well as the warning to my father.

"Thank you, thank you, thank you. You'll fix this." Yep, that went over well.

After that lovely bit of conversation, we spend the rest of our dinner discussing low-key topics and I return home in time to get eight hours of much needed beauty sleep before filming the next day.

CHAPTER TWENTY-ONE

"Good morning, Bobby," I greet my ever-present bodyguard in the morning.

"Morning, Gracie. Did you sleep well?"

"Yes, I did. How about you?"

"Great."

We lapse into silence after this witty exchange as we walk to the studio. I notice I am feeling cranky again. I think I'm tiring of my constant protector. Of course, I immediately feel guilty because he's risking his life, at least in theory, by providing the protection. I decide to try harder.

"What do you do for fun after you've protected me all day?"

"My partner and I typically just hang at our apartment, although last night, we went out to a jazz concert at the park." Partner? Jazz? Wow, he's busted all of my cop stereotypes in one statement.

"You like jazz?"

"Absolutely. Do you?"

"Um, not really. I'm more of a blues gal myself."

"Blues is good too," he comments and we smile.

The rest of the walk feels more natural but I am still beginning to feel that the era of my agreeing to protection is coming to a close. We part at the studio door.

"Hey, Georgie," I sing out as I head through security.

"Hi, Miss Gracie."

I walk, practically with a bounce in my step, to the dressing room. Man, I love my job — and not just because of a certain coworker. Danielle is again the only one in the room when I arrive. I guess the others have had a pretty light filming schedule. Or, they might be filming when I'm not here, I realize.

"Hey, Danielle," I greet her as I throw my things on the counter. "We finally get to work together."

"That's right. We're finally in the same scene." Despite nearly three weeks of filming and seeing Danielle almost every day, we have yet to have a scene together. However, the scene this morning is one involving a fairly large chunk of the town. It's a rather involved scene and the only one I'm filming today.

"Where are you and Julian going for lunch?"

"I don't know yet," I answer automatically while pulling a shirt on over my head. Oh, right, she was here yesterday when he invited me to lunch. "It's just lunch," I continue immediately.

"My, my, aren't we defensive?" She asks this with a hint of smile.

"Why do you guys keep ragging on me?" I ask almost absentmindedly while pulling on my skirt.

"Why do you let it get to you?"

"Oh, never mind," I say with a sigh. The Ice Queen saves me from further conversation.

"You're needed in hair and makeup," the PA with the icy blond hair announces and then tries to vanish. I stop her before she can leave.

"Thanks," I begin. She seems to be looking through me rather than at me. Why doesn't she like me? Seriously, everybody likes me. "I see you all the time, but I don't even know your name," I say encouragingly.

"You're needed in hair and makeup," she repeats, as though I said nothing, and this time she successfully vanishes before I can speak again.

"Thank you Ice Queen," I mumble irritably. Danielle laughs and I flush, not realizing I had said that loud enough to be heard. "Sorry, that was rude."

"No, that's perfect. Do you think she even has a name?"

"I don't know. I've never heard her introduce herself. That's why I tried to ask. Have you ever seen her smile?" Danielle shakes her head in the negative. "Are you ready?" Then we're off to hair and makeup; in fifteen minutes we're on set, ready to film.

"Any word on the trial?" Richard greets me with this question every day on set. He's really worried about the whole thing.

"Nothing yet. I'm getting tired of the bodyguard thing," I admit.

"Maybe you just need a new bodyguard."

"Are you volunteering?" I tease Richard.

"Not at all, but I bet I could guess who'd jump at the chance," he responds and his eyes veer off my face to look across the room. I know, of course, who he is looking at.

"Yeah, yeah, yeah," I say in a dismissive tone, although my gaze follows his sight line. Julian offers a wave when he sees me. I wave back, feeling, but ignoring, Richard's speculative gaze.

"You're playing with fire, Gracie," he says softly. I tear my gaze from Julian and face Richard (in more ways than one).

"How many times do I have to tell everybody? We're just friends."

"As many times as it takes to convince yourself that that's enough."

"Wow, that's deep," I say sarcastically, then immediately regret the tone. "I'm sorry. I know you mean well."

"I don't want to see either of you get hurt. Julian's really confused right now and seeing you isn't helping him. My wife and I went through a rough patch years ago and I shudder to think what might have happened if she had met someone the way Julian has met you."

"Richard, I had no idea," I say, feeling like an idiot.

"Why would you? It's okay. We worked through our issues and our marriage is even stronger than before the troubles. I really want what's best for you and Julian. I don't know what that is. Have you thought about it?"

I am saved by the bell, metaphorically speaking, as Miranda commands our attention and sets about directing this scene. We're filming a dream sequence of one character, resulting in unusual configurations of actors, but shooting goes well and soon we're finished.

"Excellent job, everybody," Miranda congratulates the group. "Let's break for lunch. Those of you who still have scenes this afternoon, you know when to be back." With that, she strides away, presumably toward her office. Julian is already heading in my direction. Richard, from across the room, notices this and manages to give me a look.

"Are we still on for lunch?"

"Of course." Screw everybody and their warnings. A man and a woman, even if they're attracted to each other, can be platonic friends. Although, as some wit once said, denial ain't just a river in Egypt.

"How about Angelica's, on 12th Street?"

"That's one of my favorite vegetarian restaurants in the city," I respond enthusiastically to the suggestion.

"Excellent. Meet out front in fifteen minutes?"

"Sounds great."

I head off to the dressing room to remove my makeup and change back into my street clothes. Maybe I am deluding myself about Julian, but until something happens, I'm not going to worry about it. After changing and gathering up my belongings, I meet Julian, and of course Bobby, out front and the three of us walk to the restaurant. To be fair, Bobby does walk a bit behind us so as to be less intrusive.

"I'll wait out front," Bobby says after inspecting Angelica's Kitchen for people out to harm me.

"Do you want us to bring you out anything?" I feel kind of bad that he has to just sit and wait, although I suppose, that is what the job entails.

"Nope, I'm good. Thanks for the offer, though."

"Sure. See you in a bit."

Julian and I catch the waitress's eye and are led to our seats. We make random idle chitchat until after we finish eating our food. I had the fabulous kinpira salad (appetizer size, of course) and Julian went all out ordering the norimaki (that's vegetarian sushi for those of you who have never been to Angelica's). Despite my infamous sweet tooth, we opt to skip the dessert today and I am beginning to feel nervous. Julian has a very intense look on his face and I'm wondering if my thoughts from earlier (you know, about being friends until something happens to question that) are about to prove prophetic. I decide to just jump in with both feet.

"You look like you've got something on your mind," I say, with only the slightest bit of trepidation.

"Yes, I do," he responds. And then he is silent, just staring.

"Would you like to share?"

"I'm trying to decide what I should say and how I should say it," he says slowly.

"Don't over think it," I reply breezily. "Just say it." I hope I don't regret that bit of encouragement.

"I know we've only known each other a few weeks," Julian begins and I can feel my heart begin to beat feverishly in my chest. "But, from the moment I saw you, I have felt drawn to you."

"Aw, that's just lust," I say in a failed attempt at levity.

"Actually, yes, the physical attraction was the start of it. Talking to you and spending time with you just intensified that initial attraction and increased it far beyond anything strictly physical."

I am speechless for possibly the first time in my life. He waits patiently for me to have some kind of reaction, so I continue to try for honesty.

"I have those same feelings…but…what about your wife?" I hate bringing her into this, but to not do so would be like ignoring the elephant in the room. A shadow flickers in his eyes.

"I don't know." I wait to see if he will elaborate on this statement but he does not.

"What do you want?"

"You," he says simply. Then he sighs. I laugh, startling him. "What was the laugh for?"

"I'm usually the one with the dramatic sighs." He chuckles. "Impossible relationships," I say, with a shake of my head.

"What?"

"I'm reminded of *Pretty Woman*, when Richard Gere's character says his specialty is impossible relationships," I explain. "That's how I feel right now."

"What do you want?" He asks me the same question.

"You, of course. But, it isn't about that."

"It isn't?"

"No, it isn't. I won't be a mistress and I don't want to be the cause of any distress," I assert.

"You're already the cause of my distress," he counters.

"You're a funny guy."

"Yeah, I try," Julian says with a smile that quickly fades. "I wouldn't want you to be a mistress. I don't know what to do. I believe that marriage is forever."

"Then doesn't that end this conversation?"

"Not if the marriage was based on a lie."

"The pregnancy."

"Yes. I don't know how I truly feel about my wife separate from her being pregnant. And, knowing that she might not have been pregnant and lied to me, leaves me wondering if I can ever trust her again."

"It sounds like you have a lot to work out between you," I begin, "without the distraction of my presence."

"No," he disagrees, looking worried.

"Yes. I can't see you again until you decide what to do."

"We can still be friends," Julian insists, though I can see in his eyes he doesn't believe his own words.

"No, we can't," I reply sadly. "The feelings are too intense and whatever the reason for your marriage, you *are* married. Those issues need to be resolved before you and I can address any of these other issues."

"We can't see each other at all?"

"I'm only on the show one more week and after that, I'll be out of your life. That has to be the way things end."

"That won't work for me," he argues.

"You don't have a choice," I tell him and stand up. I smile crookedly, needing to end this conversation before I start crying in public. "Good luck, Julian. Goodbye." I turn and leave before he has a chance to respond. As I hurry from the restaurant, I can feel the hot tears I tried and failed to suppress begin dripping down my face. Within seconds, Bobby is at my side.

"What's the matter? Did something happen? Are you okay?"

The rapid-fire questions are too much and I snap. "No. I'm not okay. I'm tired of it. I'm tired of everything. I have a man I loathe who probably wants to see me at the bottom of the river, wearing cement shoes. And I have a man I maybe could love telling me that he has intense feelings for me but doesn't know what to do about his wife. How do you think I'm doing?" I am practically race walking down the street, although Bobby easily matches my pace.

"I'm sorry, I didn't mean to upset you."

I slam to a halt and Bobby actually takes a few more steps past me. "I know. I'm sorry I blew up at you," I start and wipe the tears from my cheeks. "I just can't do it anymore."

"What do you mean?"

"This," I say with a wide arm gesture. "I need you to not be here. I need to feel safe again."

"Are you sure now is the time to make this decision? You know, when you're…not feeling yourself."

"Now is as good a time as any," I say resignedly. "Bobby, you have been great since the indictment, but I can't do it anymore. I am ready to take a chance on protecting myself."

"Even if that chance means you end up hurt or dead," Bobby says gently.

"Yes, even if it means that." I start walking again, albeit at a slower pace.

"Why don't you call Ms. Gregson?"

I realize that Bobby isn't going to go away until someone official tells him to. "Fine. I'll call her right now." I whip out my cell phone and find the assistant district attorney in my phone book. Naturally, I get her voice mail.

"Hi, Ms. Gregson. This is Gracie Corsini. You don't need to call me back. I just wanted to let you know that I am no longer in need of Officer Sanders' protective services. He has been exemplary, of course," he smiles at this, "but I need to get back to my normal life. If you could let his superiors know so that they can reassign him and his services will be put to better use.

Thank you very much for everything." I disconnect the call and replace the phone in my bag. "There. It's all taken care of. Thank you very much for everything," I say with finality, holding out my hand.

"You're most certainly welcome, Gracie. But, if it's all the same to you, I'll hang around outside your building until I get the word that I should leave."

I smile, expecting nothing less. "I kind of thought you would." We maintain a companionable silence the rest of the way home. I give him a half-wave at the door, saddened by the knowledge that he wouldn't be there in the morning, but also glad to lose my shadow.

"Jane, are you here?" I call out my question while walking through the door. Boy do we have a lot to talk about.

"Yeah, I'm in the bathroom." She pokes her head around the bathroom door and I can see her hair is wrapped in a towel. "Give me five minutes to finish up." The door closes behind her.

"Okay," I respond needlessly before heading to my room to throw down my backpack. I am sitting on the couch eating chocolate-chip cookie-dough ice cream straight from the half-gallon container when Jane enters the living room a few minutes later.

"Uh-oh," she says, eyeing the ice cream. "You didn't even bother with a bowl. This can't be good."

"Oh, no, everything's fine," I say in a chipper tone. Jane retreats to the kitchen and returns with a spoon of her own.

"What's up?" She asks, already digging her spoon into the container I'm still clutching like a safety raft.

"Where to begin? I fired Bobby. I suppose I can start there," I say listlessly.

"You fired Bobby? Can you even do that? What about Tommy?"

"Of course I can do that. It's my life and if I don't want protection, it can't be forced on me," I insist.

"Sure, I guess," she agrees, sounding uncertain. "Why would you want to make yourself a target?"

"I'm already a target," I point out.

"True, but now you're an unprotected one."

"It'll be fine." Yum, this ice cream is good.

"I'm still confused," Jane continues. "Why did you actually fire him? On some kind of principle?"

"I'd been thinking about it for a couple of days. The timing just seemed right today," I explain vaguely.

"Something must have happened. What haven't you told me?" Perceptive woman, my roommate.

"I had lunch with Julian today," I tell her.

"Ah-ha. I knew it!"

"Knew what?"

"That there was more to the story. What happened at lunch?"

"Same old, same old. Julian said he had feelings for me, but believes marriage is forever." I am really going to town on the ice cream, talking between mouthfuls. Most of the time, anyway.

"He finally said it. Tell me you weren't really surprised by any of that."

"Well," I falter.

"Oh, c'mon, Gracie. You're smarter than that. Everyone knows the two of you are at least physically attracted to each other. How can you be surprised it became more?" Jane sounds exasperated.

"Alright, already. You're right. I had my suspicions. I guess I was hoping…I don't know what I was hoping for," I finish with a sigh and dig out a heaping spoonful of the delectable ice cream.

"Good grief. Tell me exactly what was said," Jane demands and I comply. When I finish, it is Jane's turn to sigh.

"So, after that conversation, you got upset, ran into Bobby, and fired him, right?"

"More or less." Ugh, maybe I've had enough ice cream. I push it toward Jane, who spoons herself some more before replacing the lid.

"Gracie, what are you doing?" As Jane is bringing the ice cream to the kitchen, I cannot see her face, but that exasperated tone is still present.

"Digesting ice cream."

"Smart ass. You want to try again?"

"I don't know what I'm doing. I thought I was protecting myself by having Bobby and being just friends with Julian."

Jane actually laughs at my statement, though not meanly. "This is how you protect yourself? You fire your bodyguard and you utterly fail at being *just friends* with Julian."

"Thanks for the summary." I bury my face in a couch cushion. "What should I do?" I mumble my question.

"I wouldn't worry too much about Bobby."

I raise my head. "No?"

"Wasn't he only going to be able to stay for a few weeks anyway?"

"Good point. And Julian?"

"I think it's clear the two of you can't be just friends."

"Indeed," I comment, eyes closed, head tilted back.

"You were right to tell him you couldn't see him anymore."

"Then why doesn't it feel right?" I ask this and immediately feel my face flush and my eyes moisten. Oh, crap, I'm going to cry again. This does not go unnoticed by Jane, whose tone noticeably softens when she continues.

"Because you like him as more than a friend. As a lot more than a friend, I'm guessing."

"Yeah, I guess that's it." The urge to cry is passing. "It's so weird, though."

"What?"

"I've only known him a few weeks. I never thought you could fall for someone so quickly."

"Where do you think the phrase 'love at first sight' comes from?"

"Yeah, but I always chalked that up to lust at first sight."

Jane laughs, then grows serious. "Will you be able to avoid him at work? You have, what, a week and a half left?"

"Yes and yes to your questions," I answer. "We rarely have scenes together and unless he seeks me out, I don't usually run into him, even when we have overlapping call times."

"That's good. I say, get through the rest of the filming and move on with your life," Jane offers as her final piece of advice.

"I'll do my best," I say with a genuine smile. "I have two more days of filming this week and two next week. I can do this."

"Yes, you can!" Jane's such a great cheerleader.

I do feel better, but why do I still feel so unsure?

CHAPTER TWENTY-TWO

When I leave my apartment building the next day, I instinctively look for Bobby. Then I remember I fired him. I feel sadness and a pang of regret for an instant. Honestly, his services are better used somewhere else.

The walk to the studio is quieter without Bobby, and I find myself missing the companionship. Forget it, I tell myself as I reach the studio. I breeze through security and am in the dressing room changing when Danielle and Kris arrive.

"How was lunch?"

"It was fine, Danielle. How are you today?" I keep my tone light, but am hopeful that my pointed reply will not go unnoticed. It doesn't.

"I'm doing fabulous. Today is going to be a great day. Right, Kris?"

"Definitely." Luckily, Kris apparently missed the pointed quality in my and Danielle's exchange.

Since I am a naturally happy person, I find that the funk from the past 24 hours is lifting and the women's good mood is contagious.

Filming goes well and I am still feeling fine when Richard stops me as I'm leaving for the day. "Did something happen yesterday?"

"What do you mean?"

"With Julian."

"Why do you ask me?"

"Have you seen him today?"

"No, I haven't. What is this about?"

"He seems to have woken up on the wrong side of the bed this morning," Richard explains, and for some inexplicable reason, I feel guilty.

"Why would you think I have anything to do with that? Has anyone asked his wife?" Watch the tone, Gracie.

Richard gives me a look. "That answers my question."

"Look, everyone was right. We can't be just friends. We realized that yesterday."

"I'm sorry, Gracie," Richard says with feeling. "I know you really like him."

"Yeah, well, I don't want to get hurt. Anymore than I already have," I add.

"I think you guys made the right decision."

"Thanks."

"He has issues he needs to work out. And, who knows what may happen…"

"I'm going to live my life and let the future take care of itself," I declare.

"Good for you, Gracie. Anyway, sorry to hold you up."

"No worries, Richard."

"I'll see you next week."

"You're not filming tomorrow?"

"Nope."

"See you Monday, then." I walk toward the exit as Richard walks back toward his dressing room. While I'm sorry to hear

Julian is upset, there isn't anything I can do about it, so I try to forget it.

The next day's filming passes in a blur. So far, so good, I think to myself as I leave the studio. I've managed to avoid Julian both days of filming and only have two more days left next week. I should feel pretty successful. Why do I feel such a sense of regret?

Thankfully, the ringing of my cell phone interrupts that most unhelpful line of thinking. I glance at the screen and, recognizing the number of the district attorney's office, immediately decline to answer.

Whatever Ms. Gregson has to say, she can leave it in a message. If Tommy flipped or not, a message can convey that information. If she's calling about Bobby, I really don't want to hear it. After about a minute, the phone chirps that I have a new message. I unlock the phone and select my new voice message.

"Hello, Ms. Corsini. This is Aliana Gregson calling. I've heard that you no longer require protective services. Obviously, that's your decision, although I do wish you had discussed it with me first. Anyway, I have important news regarding the case. Please call me at your earliest convenience." She recites her number and then disconnects the call.

I delete the message and pop the phone into my backpack. Her tone was not suggestive of good news and I'd just as soon delay hearing bad. I'll call her tomorrow. Just then, I sense a presence before me.

Oh, the irony. I gaze into the smug, vaguely threatening countenance of my favorite drug lord, Tommy Pullman. "Hi, Tommy," I greet him with as much indifference as I can muster and move to walk around him. He seems about to impede my path, thinks better of the maneuver (perhaps recalling our last encounter), and falls into step beside me.

"Hi, Gracie. How's it going?"

Oh, goody, small talk with a gangsta. "It's going well. How are you?"

"I'm doing well on this grand day."

I squint at him, trying to decipher his game, and he grins broadly at me. "Why is that?"

"I guess you haven't heard." He pauses.

"Heard what?" I ask somewhat perfunctorily, although I am curious. I'm thinking of the call from Aliana Gregson that I didn't take.

"I won't bore you with the details, but there's been problems with the case against me. You're all that's left."

My heart skips a beat. "What are you talking about?"

"Just what I said. The case has been reduced to he said-she said. And, you know the unreliability of eyewitness testimony."

"Studying those law books again," I say dryly.

"It pays to be well-educated. Besides the evaporation of the case, witnesses recant or," his eyes narrow though a fixed smile remains, "witnesses disappear."

I break off eye contact and although I continue to walk, my insides feel still, almost frozen. I look back over at him. "Is that a threat?" I ask quietly.

Tommy's face transforms into a mask of contriteness. "Of course not. You must have misunderstood my point."

"I guess I did," I retort with a hint of anger creeping into my voice.

"I was just informing you about the finer points of the law and what it means for such a weak case."

"Consider your message delivered," I say, my voice filled now with a cold fury. How dare he threaten me! "Only keep in mind, weak or not, I never back down — and you're going to jail." I abruptly smile brightly and even laugh; this results in a look of confusion from Tommy, as well as a brief flash of anger in his eyes. "You should leave now." And, amazingly, with a small nod of his head, he melts away into the throng of passers-by.

Could my life be any more surreal and dramatic? I ask myself as I retrieve my cell phone from my backpack and autodial the district attorney's office. Guess I better find out just what Tommy was talking about.

I quickly get Ms. Gregson on the phone. "I just missed your call. What's the news?" I chatter breezily.

"Let me reiterate that I wish you had spoken with me first before relieving your protective officer," she begins and I jump in before she can continue.

"Ms. Gregson, Bobby wasn't going to be able to guard me forever. I didn't think it was a big deal to let him go a few days or maybe a couple of weeks before he would have been reassigned anyway. Can you tell me what's going on with the case? Your message didn't sound promising."

I hear a soft sigh from her end of the line. "There have been some new developments." She pauses.

"Yes?"

"We've decided to drop the charges," she finally states.

"What?"

"We've had difficulties with other aspects of the case and when it came right down to it, you're the only witness or even evidence we have remaining."

"And I'm not enough," I say flatly. This sucks.

"Unfortunately, no. We were unable to convince Mr. Pullman to testify against his boss."

"That's too bad. But, I thought you said we had a reasonably good case, albeit largely circumstantial."

"That's true, but with these... difficulties, even the circumstantial evidence is not available to us."

This whole conversation was maddening. "What happened?"

Another sigh. "I'm not at liberty to discuss the specifics."

"Fine. Whatever. Does Tommy know the charges have been dropped?"

"He will shortly. We're filing the paperwork today."

"That's good, given that he and I just had the most lovely chat," I say offhand, as though it is no big deal that a gangster drug dealer was chatting with me on the sidewalk.

"What?" She asks with a sharp intake of breath.

I recount the conversation as best as I can. "He never really threatened me, but the meaning was clear."

"We'd never prove the conversation was meant to intimidate. At any rate, that should be the last you see of him, once his attorney informs him that the case has been dropped."

"I certainly hope so." It might suck that the charges were dropped, but at least the silver lining is that I'm no longer any kind of threat to him. I realize that Ms. Gregson has still been speaking. "I'm sorry," I interrupt, "I missed that."

"I was apologizing for putting you through all of this stress for nothing."

She sounds genuinely contrite and I notice I'm not even angry. "It's not your fault. You did everything you could. Honestly, it's not like he's going to stop doing what he's doing. You'll get him next time."

"I'm sure we will," she agrees and I can hear the smile in her voice. "If anything changes, I'll contact you, but otherwise I think you can safely conclude that your involvement with the district attorney's office has come to a close."

"Thanks for everything and good luck."

"Good luck to you, too, Gracie." The line disconnects and I put my phone away. I have an odd feeling of unfinished business now, but simply shrug it off. It's over; there's nothing I can do about it. Time to move on to bigger and better things. Starting with the wrap of filming on the soap opera… and avoiding Julian for two last days. Oy.

*****

"Good morning, George," I sing out to the security guard as I waltz through the foyer of the studio building and walk toward my dressing room. None of my roommates are present when I arrive. I toss my backpack on the counter and turn toward my wardrobe for the scenes today. I have only two, both designed for the final preparation of my great-grandmother Lily's 100th birthday party. As I recall from my script, one of the scenes is with Richard and the other is in the restaurant arranging the setting for the party. Julian is not in either scene so I do not anticipate difficulty avoiding him today. Tomorrow will be a different story, but I plan to worry about tomorrow, tomorrow. Right now, I focus on my wardrobe. It's pretty basic for the scene with Richard – jeans and a teal turtleneck. I slip into these, head to hair and makeup, and am quickly sitting in Richard's "living room" waiting to begin the scene.

"Good morning, Janie," Richard says, taking a seat beside me on the couch.

"Morning, Max," I respond with a smile. The scene is a fairly short one, where my brother and I discuss the party. It gets much more exciting after I leave and his current love interest comes in and tells him she's pregnant by another man. Ooh, gotta love those soap triangles.

"How goes the court case?"

"That's so yesterday," I reply in my Valley-girl tone and laugh. "Actually, it really is. The case was dismissed."

"What happened?" Richard looks shocked. I summarize the pertinent details. "Damn, that sucks."

"My sentiments exactly."

"Does that mean he gets away with everything?"

I shrug. "Apparently so."

Richard is about to speak again when Miranda enters the set. When the director arrives and makes a beeline for you, you tend to be quiet.

"Oh, good. You're both here," she says, speaking rapidly. "This scene shouldn't be too difficult and I'm hoping to knock it out with a minimum number of takes. Sound good?" We both murmur our agreement and she continues speaking, telling us where she wants us for our marks. I'll spare you more boring set talk. Suffice it to say that her desire comes true and we complete our scene, including all of the various angles, fairly quickly.

"That was great, guys. Gracie, I'll see you after lunch. Richard, take five before we do your next scene," Miranda directs us before bustling back off set. We hear her mumbling something about lighting.

"Gracie, before you go, can I talk to you?"

"Of course. What's up?"

Richard's face takes on a somber look and he lowers his voice. "Have you spoken to Julian?"

"No. I told you. We're staying away from each other. Why?"

"I was just wondering."

"You can't ask me that and then not tell me why," I object.

"It's no big deal. I was just curious," Richard insists.

I am about to continue arguing but there is something about his expression that causes me to pause. I ask a question instead. "He's okay, right? You'd tell me if something had happened."

"Absolutely. He's fine," Richard reassures me. "I'll see you after lunch for the restaurant scene." I take the dismissal hint and depart with a small wave.

Back in the dressing room, all three of the other women have arrived. They are in various stages of undress when I enter the room. We exchange greetings and I turn to my clothing. I plan to slip back into my street clothes until after lunch. I've found that it is not a good idea to eat in your wardrobe. I sense eyes on me and look into my mirror. My gaze locks onto Danielle's. I ask a silent *What?* and she shakes her head slightly. My mind reading may not be perfected yet, but I'm guessing she wants to talk to me after the other women leave. I've changed into my street clothes and am wolfing down lunch while reviewing lines for the later scene by the time the other two women finish up and depart.

"What's up?" I ask Danielle. The redhead walks over and takes an empty seat closer to me.

"When's the last time you spoke to Julian?"

"A week," I respond. "What's going on? Richard asked me about Julian earlier."

"What did he tell you?" She seems unusually cautious.

"Nothing. Please don't you do the same. You guys can't ask me about him like this and then leave me hanging. Please."

I see uncertainty in her blue eyes, but she apparently decides to tell me. "Julian missed a couple of days of filming last week. Luckily they weren't too difficult to write him out of, but it's not good." I wait for the *and.* "And then on Friday, Richard and I overheard him on his cell phone." Again, I wait for her to continue. She doesn't.

"What? Did you hear something…bad?"

Danielle breaks eye contact before answering. "Julian moved out."

It takes a second for that to sink in. My eyes widen just as Danielle resumes eye contact. "You mean?"

"I don't know what it means," she hastens to add. "All we know is that he is not living with his wife right now."

My eyes narrow. "You and Richard thought maybe I played an active role in that decision," I say in an accusatory tone. Danielle looks embarrassed.

"We didn't know," she says defensively. "We thought, maybe." Her sentence abruptly ends.

"I can see why you guys might think that," I say, softening my tone. "But, I promise you both that I had nothing to do with that decision. At least not directly," I clarify. Danielle seems relieved.

"Good. I mean, I figured that was the case, but it's nice to hear it from you." She smiles her brilliant smile then. I return the smile and am glad that this is settled.

Sheesh, just because a guy decides to leave his wife, doesn't mean you had anything to do with it. Of course, the fact that I feel a glimmer of possibility for the two of us betrays my innermost feelings on the matter. I squish those feelings and, having finished lunch, change into my jeans and a different long-sleeve top for the afternoon, since the prep scene ostensibly takes place the next day, the same day as the party.

After lunch, when I arrive on the restaurant set, I almost immediately run into Richard.

"I'm sorry, Gracie."

"For what?" I ask, although I know the answer.

"I spoke to Danielle. I never should have doubted your word."

"Thank you."

"When you said you'd let him work things out for himself, I should have realized you meant it," he continues.

"It's okay, Richard," I assure him, mainly because I'm worried he'll continue to apologize. "It's like I told Danielle. I can see why you'd think I might have been directly involved. But, I'd like to think that after you confided about the difficulties you faced in your own marriage, you would know that I wouldn't take my potential influence in Julian's life lightly."

Richard smiles. "Of course. So, you're not mad?"

"Dude, you sound like a girl," I can't help but say and he laughs. "Of course, I'm not mad. Next time, just ask me if you're concerned about something."

"I will," he assures me.

Miranda arrives then and we get down to business, filming

the preparation scenes for the party we'll be filming tomorrow. The remainder of the day is uneventful and I'm feeling pretty good when I leave. Naturally, I have trouble sleeping that night. My subconscious knows it will be impossible to completely avoid Julian tomorrow during the party scene. My character is one of the hosts, so at some point she speaks to almost everyone in town, including Julian's character.

Despite tossing and turning all night, I wake up before my alarm. I arrive at the studio even earlier than I normally do. Of course, I recognize that this is due to nervous energy because I'm going to see and speak to Julian for the first time in over a week. I arrive at the empty dressing room and slip into my party duds. A fabulous sleeveless, empire-waist dress made of a satiny material, falling in a fitted but soft wave of chocolate brown to about an inch above the knee. Not my usual color, but once I slid the dress over my head, I could see the wisdom of the designer. I looked hot – but still demure enough to be appropriate for my great-grandmother's 100th birthday party.

Once I'm ready, I review my dialogue while I wait for everyone else to arrive. I studiously avoid any thoughts of Julian. I'll admit I'm only partially successful. The other women in my dressing room filter in one by one and soon it's time to head to hair and makeup.

The set bustles with crew and cast members. Since my character's great-grandmother, Lily, is practically the matriarch of the town, nearly every actor on the show is in this scene to a greater or lesser extent. I see Richard and head in his direction. Alas, I am waylaid before I can arrive at my destination.

"Hi, Gracie," comes a soft, familiar voice to my right.

"Hi, Julian," I respond and smile up at him. Damn, he's hot. I notice his eyes look sad, though, and my smile slips slightly.

"How have you been?"

"I've been good. How have you been?"

"Okay." He pauses, looks away, before continuing. "I've missed you."

My heart skips a beat. "I've missed you, too," I admit, unsure if I should be honest, knowing what Richard and Danielle have told me.

His face brightens and I feel guilty, like I've been deliberately causing him heartache. "Can we talk after the shoot?"

No, no, no! Well, not unless you're leaving your wife, is what I instantly think. "Of course," is what I actually say.

"I'll talk to you then."

Julian walks off, to be replaced almost instantaneously by Richard.

"What was that all about?"

"He wants to talk."

"Are you going to?"

I give Richard my most exaggerated eye roll. "Of course. Why wouldn't I?"

"Oh, I don't know. Because he may have just left his wife last week and is still in emotional turmoil."

That gives me pause and I am less sure of myself when I retort. "We're just going to talk."

"You know what? I'll quit interfering," Richard suddenly says. "Things will be different after today anyway, since today is your last day."

"Yes, it is," I respond, beginning to feel sad.

"If I don't see you after the shoot, it's been great working with you," Richard says, almost shyly.

I throw my arms around him. "You've been a great big brother. I'm really going to miss you."

"I'm going to miss you, too. Be careful with everything," he says warningly. "You know what I mean."

"Okay, everybody, let's get this done," comes a loud female voice behind us and I am once again saved from an uncomfortable conversation by Miranda. She begins directing (hence her title, right?) everyone where to stand and slowly as the hours pass, we shoot every last scene of that birthday party. It takes the entire day and I am exhausted when she finally announces we're finished.

"That's a wrap."

Despite the exhaustion, I am filled with nervous energy over my pending conversation with Julian. Good grief, you'd think we were dating. I quit thinking about it and head for the dressing room to change into my street clothes.

Danielle, Kris, and Megan have beaten me back to the room and are already changing out of their wardrobe. I close the door behind me and begin changing.

"Today's your last day, right, Gracie?" Kris suddenly asks. Danielle and Megan stop what they're doing and face me.

"That's right, I forgot," Danielle states.

"We're going to miss you, Gracie," Megan says and the others chime in with similar sentiments.

"I'm going to miss you guys, too." I'm feeling emotional again. The women approach me and we exchange hugs.

"Who knows? Maybe you'll be back in six months for a guest appearance," Danielle offers and the others nod.

"That would be cool," Megan adds.

"Yeah, it would," I agree. Now that the good-byes have been offered, it feels awkward to still be there. The others finish packing their belongings and quickly leave. I take my time, unsure if I am prolonging my experience at the studio or trying to avoid my conversation with Julian. Probably both.

If the latter was my intention, that attempt is thwarted by a knock on the partially closed door. It opens wider and I turn to see Julian standing on the threshold.

"Hey, Julian," I greet him warmly. There's no reason this conversation can't go well, I've decided.

"Hey, Gracie. I know today is your last day, so I wanted to talk to you before you left."

"Of course. Come on in," I invite, and gesture at the many vacated seats. He chooses the closest one to me. I can already feel the physical heat between us. "What did you want to talk about?" I ask this more so that I can focus on something other than the attraction between us than because I don't know the answer. He ignores the obviousness of my question and rather than comment on it, actually answers it.

"I'd like to talk about the restaurant."

Believe it or not, I am momentarily confused and then realize he's talking about when I fled the restaurant in emotional agony. "Oh, that," I say nonchalantly.

Julian smiles. "I know admitting we have feelings for each other was hard," he begins.

"Because you're married," I remind him.

"Yes, because I'm married," he agrees. "I've never had feelings for someone like this before. I ache for you everyday we're not together. This last week has been terrible."

"I'm sorry," I say and am genuinely unhappy that his feelings for me have caused this much pain.

He shakes off my apology. "That's not the point. I don't know what to do about this," he finally admits helplessly.

"What do you want from me?"

"I don't know. How strong are your feelings for me?"

"Pretty strong," I acknowledge, though I've noted we are steadfastly avoiding use of the L-word.

"What do you want?" he asks me, as he had before in the restaurant.

I decide to go all in. "I want you," I answer with the barest honesty I can muster. It is difficult maintaining eye contact. I feel like we're about to bore holes into each other's skulls with the intensities of our gazes.

"Yeah, me too," he agrees quietly. He reaches out to take my hands in his and, lord help me, I let him.

"What about your wife?" I try to inject some reality into this conversation.

"I've moved out."

"And?"

"And what?"

"Are you planning to… divorce?" I hesitate to push, but if we're going no-holds-barred here, then this is it.

I can feel the pressure of his hands on mine before he answers. "I don't know. I told you how important the bonds of marriage are to me."

"Then nothing really has changed," I conclude sadly and withdraw my hands from his.

"What do you mean? I've taken a step. I moved out," he insists with boyish sincerity.

"I realize that. But, you're still married and I can't be involved with a married man," I insist, though I can feel my resolve weakening.

I don't know if he could sense the change in my demeanor, but there he is, leaning in to kiss me. I don't fight him off, try to stop him in any way. Instead, I allow his lips to touch mine, softly then with more pressure. The kiss is sweet, almost chaste, but still sends shock waves through my body. If this keeps up, I won't be able to construct a coherent thought. And that's not good.

Abruptly, I pull back. "No!" I say this with more intensity than planned. He looks startled, his eyes still heavy with desire. "I can't do this, I just can't. I'm sorry, Julian." I stand up and begin gathering up the last of my belongings. Julian is saying something at my back, but I can't seem to hear him through the crashing waves in my skull. I realize that I'm crying again. I turn to face him and my tears stop his flow of words.

"Julian, you know how I feel. That isn't going to change any time soon. But we were right the other day when we decided to stay apart. If you think there's even a chance for your marriage, then we can't see each other. If you decide that your marriage is over and that what we have is too important, then get a divorce and give me a call. Otherwise, I don't ever want to see you again."

I push past him before he can think to say anything and am out the door and down the hall before I hear him calling my name. I walk faster. I don't know if he has chosen to follow me, but I reach security without incident and push through the double doors. I am already charging down the sidewalk when it registers that George called out my name as I went past.

I am lucky not to get killed as I jaywalk left and right and push my way onto the subway car. I am oblivious to the stares, some appearing concerned, though nobody says anything, and eventually I reach my apartment door.

"Hey, Gracie, how was the last day of filming?" Jane manages to ask this entire question as I'm pushing through the front door. The smile immediately falls from her face when she sees my tear-stained cheeks and puffy, red-rimmed eyes. "Oh my God, what happened?" She rushes to my side and I collapse into her arms.

"I can't believe I'm being such a girl about this," I sob, honestly feeling like an idiot.

"Being a girl about what?" Jane asks this as she maneuvers us over to the couch.

I sit, staring morosely ahead and fill Jane in on what was said between Julian and myself.

"Oh, Gracie, I'm so sorry. I can't even imagine how that must have been for you," she tells me.

"I really barely know him. I can't believe this is affecting me so strongly."

"Love is strange," Jane quips.

"Love? Who said anything about love?"

"You're kidding, right?"

"What do you mean? Didn't you hear me say I barely know him," I halfheartedly argue. Jane smiles sympathetically.

"I don't care if you know someone for a day or 10 years. When it's love, you know. This is how you act when you can't have it," she says, gesturing at me.

"That makes me sound…I don't know," I sigh, as I am unable to finish the thought.

"You know what I mean."

"Yeah, I know. I don't know why I'm so surprised, anyway."

"He moved out of his home, away from his wife," Jane reminds me.

"That's true. After Richard and Danielle told me he had moved out, I felt this tiny flicker of hope. But, he's still so indecisive."

"Why don't you try looking at it from another perspective? He's serious about his wedding vows." I look at her in confusion. "No, really, it's a good thing that he isn't quick to throw away his marriage," she continues.

"I guess," I say uncertainly. "Actually, you're right." I brighten at the thought. "It shows that he takes his commitments seriously."

"Exactly."

My expression turns dour again. "Of course, he's staying serious with the wrong woman."

"That may be true."

"I mean, she lied to him," I assert.

"That appears to be the case."

"How can he stay with her?"

"I don't know."

I bury my head in my hands. "I'm torturing myself with this,"

I mumble.

"What?"

I lift my head. "I said, I'm torturing myself with this."

"That would also appear to be the case."

Something about the way Jane states that strikes me as funny and I begin laughing. Jane joins in, probably just relieved that I'm not openly sobbing anymore, but her laughter trails off as mine takes on a hysterical edge.

"Gracie?"

Tears are running down my face from the laughter, not sadness, but I can see that Jane is worried about my reaction. I wave a hand at her. "It's okay. It's okay," I assure her, though she does not look particularly reassured. She waits patiently until my laughter and my tears dry up.

"Now what?" Jane asks.

"I'm going to Los Angeles." Until I say the words, I had not been fully sure what my plan would be. After uttering them, I am convinced that this is the right thing for me to do.

"What?" Jane clearly did not read my train of thought on this one.

"It's all too much," I begin. "Christopher and Alicia. Tommy. Julian," I finish softly.

"And going to LA will cure all of that?" Jane sounds skeptical.

"Cure? Probably not. But, it will get me away from all of this. Don't worry about the rent, I can still take care of that."

Jane looks hurt. "As if that would be my primary concern."

"I'm sorry," I say contritely.

"I just want you to be happy. And if going to California," she says it like a dirty word, "will do that, then by all means, leave tomorrow."

"That might be a bit too soon," I say with a chuckle, "but you have the right idea. Thanks," I add.

"For what?"

"For just being you, and being there with me through everything this year."

"What are friends for?"

I smile. "I hope Renata feels the same way."

This confuses Jane. "Who?"

"My friend Renata who doesn't know she's going to be hosting me during my trip to Los Angeles."

"I'm sure she won't mind."

I retrieve my cell phone from my backpack and autodial Renata. "I guess we'll see," I say to Jane as the phone rings 3000 miles away.

"Hey, girl," I say with considerable enthusiasm when Renata answers the phone.

"Gracie! Long time no talk. About time you called me back. What's up?"

"I need a break from the city," I begin without preamble.

"Are you coming out here?"

"If you'll have me."

"Naturally."

"Excellent. You rock, girl."

"When are you coming?"

"As soon as I get things straightened out on this end. Oh, and after I tell my family," I add as an afterthought, realizing that my mother will kill me if I leave without a family dinner first. I inwardly sigh at the notion.

"You haven't told your mother yet?" Renata attended the University of California at Los Angeles with me. She met my mother when I moved in and out of the city. That was enough to be aware of the risks of the evil eye my mother perfected.

I laugh. "I'm going to, I promise."

"She'll kill me, too, just for helping you, if you don't give her a heads up," Renata says in a warning tone.

Not that she can see it, but I raise my free hand in mock surrender. "I know, I know. I swear I will not board the plane before telling her."

"In person."

"In person," I repeat, feeling like maybe we need to do a cross-country pinky swear before Renata will believe me.

"Okay, sounds cool. Ring me when you have the flight info and I will pick you up at the airport."

"Will do. Talk later." We terminate the call and I turn to face Jane. "Want to go to family dinner on Saturday?"

She smiles. Jane loves my family and they'll be thrilled to see her so soon after the last family dinner. "Absolutely."

CHAPTER TWENTY-THREE

It's Saturday night. My flight leaves for California first thing tomorrow morning. My mother hates when I go anywhere for a long time and I suspect I'll be in LA for at least a month, more likely two or three. I think I'll leave it open-ended with her, however. I'll be more specific regarding the length of my stay once I've gotten settled in with Renata. I'm just being courteous, you understand. I wouldn't want to give my mother incorrect information. Besides, she can't kill me long distance.

"Tell her after dinner," Jane suggests, as I open the front door of my parents' home. I immediately hear my brother and sister in separate conversations with my father and mother, respectively.

"How do they always get here before me?" I stage whisper to Jane as we walk through the doorway. Jane does not answer me, instead sniffing the air like a dog, trying to determine tonight's entrée.

"Because we know how to be on time," my brother replies instead. I very maturely stick my tongue out at him and he laughs. He and our father pause in their conversation to greet us properly and then resume their talk about the New England Patriots. My father is a fan, my brother is not. Jane and I continue through to the kitchen, joining my mother and sister, who are sitting at the table.

"That smells wonderful, Annabella," Jane comments, heading immediately toward the stove. My mother rises and joins her over the bubbling contents of the various pots and pans. I sit next to my sister, who leans over conspiratorially.

"Have you said anything?" She asks this quietly, but it is a small kitchen and I'm amazed that our mother doesn't seem to hear. Since she knows nothing about Los Angeles, I assume she means her modeling contract.

"No Maria, not yet," I whisper back.

She starts to add something but stops when I give her a sharp jerk of my head in the universal sign to *shut up*. This does not go unnoticed by my mother.

"What are you doing? Telling secrets?" My mother fixes a stare on us that would make any interrogator proud. I look pointedly at Maria before answering.

"Of course we are," I confirm brightly. My mother is not a moron, so why try to lie? Maria gasps and my mother's eyes narrow. "All will be revealed in due course." I smile at my mother and avoid eye contact with my sister, though I sense her mouth is likely agape. Hey, it was the best non-lie non-answer I could think of. Even Jane, standing next to my mother, looks like she wants to edge out of the kitchen to the relative safety of the living room.

Naturally, my brother and father choose right then to appear in the kitchen doorway. "That smells great, mama," Anthony enthuses, then notices the unspoken tension.

"It'll be another ten minutes," my mother informs him, apparently (to the great surprise of the ladies in the room) deciding to let the questioning go. With a quick glance at me, she returns to stirring the meal and speaking with Jane. Maria and I look at each other and I have to stifle the urge to giggle. Maria abruptly rises.

"I'll set the table," she announces. Conversations resume, but everything seems awkward when at last the food is complete and we're all seated around the table. I wait until we've just about finished before I speak the unspoken.

"I'm leaving for Los Angeles tomorrow," I announce.

"Going to visit Renata?" Anthony (correctly) assumes.

"Yes," I answer, without elaboration.

"When will you be back?" My mother asks this and I know not to provide another non-answer.

"I don't know," I answer truthfully. "I'm going to try to get some work out there. I'll be gone for certainly a month, probably more like two." Or three, I finish silently.

My mother says nothing, but my father takes it in stride. "What do you think you will do?"

I explain to the family about pilot season and that seems to satisfy everyone, including my mother who, while not happy, at least appears mollified. That was easy.

"Have you met a nice girl yet?" My mother turns the conversation to my brother.

"Not in the past week," Anthony answers with a laugh.

"You need to meet a nice girl," my mother insists and I tune out while they continue to verbally volley.

I'm drawn back in to the conversation when I notice Maria making frantic eye gestures at me. I can't explain it any better than that, but it worked.

"I told you about the contract," Maria says to my parents. I hear the distress in her voice and I jump in to help.

"Isn't it great?" I say with maybe a touch too much enthusiasm. Anthony raises an eyebrow, but Maria appears relieved. Big sis to the rescue.

"She has quit school," my father intones in a voice others would use to report a death.

"True," I concede, "but this contract is amazing. She's going to be on television. And, she's going to be a cover girl." Dang, I had them with television and lost them with cover girl. "You know, the magazines with the pretty women on them," I begin to explain. "That's going to be Maria." My sister looks so grateful, I'm almost embarrassed. The confusion clears on my father's face, replaced by…anger?

"No! Maria will not be naked." My father looks seriously pissed, but now we're confused.

"What?" Asks my mother.

"Papa, no," insists Maria. She is near tears.

Jane wisely stays quiet.

Anthony bursts out laughing and a half-second later, I join him. The others stare at us in astonishment.

"Um, papa, I don't believe Gracie meant those kinds of magazines with the pretty women on them," Anthony tries to explain. Maria flushes bright red as the implication hits home.

"Right," I pick up the thread. "We're talking about fashion magazines, papa, like *Elle*, *Vogue*, and *Cosmopolitan*."

Finally, understanding abounds and even my father smiles.

"This is good," he states.

"This is very good," I assure him and Maria is looking at me like I walk on water. Sheesh, I almost blew the whole thing. I check out of the conversation again as Maria explains all of the details she had told me earlier. Once my parents acknowledge the wonderful opportunity, the remainder of the evening passes without incident. I can only fervently hope I will have as much opportunity in Los Angeles. Of course, just being away from Christopher, Alicia, Tommy, and (sigh) Julian will give me a much-needed mental break.

WEST COAST

CHAPTER TWENTY-FOUR

Ahh. The West Coast – where the sun shines 364 days a year. And on the 365th day, there are mudslides or earthquakes. But, what a small price to pay to live in Heaven. I can't believe it took me this long to get back here.

"Gracie!"

I hear Renata Harvey before I see her and smile at the sound of her voice. She comes into view moments later on the waiting side of the security barrier at Los Angeles International Airport. I quicken my pace once I see her.

"Renata!" I return the greeting seconds before I reach where she's standing and we embrace. She notes that all I'm carrying is my stalwart backpack.

"Baggage claim?"

"Baggage claim," I concur. We begin our trek to where the infernally rotating conveyors of bags are kept. I had checked two rather large bags and was simply hoping they would both be there to be retrieved.

"How was your flight?"

"We didn't crash. That's always a good start," I say with a laugh.

"Smart aleck."

"Turbulence wasn't great, but I didn't hurl."

"Good."

"Oh, and I'd already seen the in-flight movie."

"That sucks. What was it? Worth watching again?"

"*Fracture*, with Anthony Hopkins."

"Isn't that *Sir* Anthony Hopkins?" she interrupts.

"Whatever," I wave off the interruption. "It's a good movie, but once you know what happens," I finish with a shrug.

"I'm so glad you're here," she unexpectedly squeals and gives me a hug.

"Me too. We're going to have so much fun!"

We continue to chat idly while we retrieve my bags (both accounted for, thank you Airport Gods) and walk to her car, parked waaay in the back of short-term parking.

"Good thing we're young and healthy," I quip.

"Seriously. I couldn't believe how crowded the parking was. It's a Sunday."

"Yeah, but it's LAX."

"Good point," she admits as we reach her brand new Toyota Prius. She unlocks the doors and pops the trunk.

"Nice car."

"Thanks."

"Is it teal?"

"Yep," she says proudly. "When your father owns a successful dealership, it's not that hard to get an impossible-to-get color."

"Perks are nice."

"Indeed."

"I'm guessing you didn't pay sticker." Having placed the bags in the back seat, we hop in the front.

"What do you think?" Renata asks with a laugh. I laugh in return. We have a lovely chat as we pop on the 405 (simply a breeze on a Sunday) and quickly arrive at her gorgeous Spanish-style two-bedroom, two-bathroom home on the outskirts of Beverly Hills. And this wasn't courtesy of her father's money. Although she continues to temp as a paralegal for the variety, Renata is a highly successful model. She's 5'10", no more than 115 pounds soaking wet, with beautiful caramel skin, amazing hazel eyes, and close cropped dark brown hair. I sometimes feel like a midget when I'm with her, but we always have fun.

Renata and I grab my bags out of the trunk and carry them inside her home. We walk through the marble foyer down a short hallway to the right, where the guest bedroom is located. We set the bags next to the walk-in closet door.

"I'll go make us some drinks while you unpack. Mimosa or screwdriver?"

"Mimosa – this is a celebration, after all."

"For sure."

Renata heads for the kitchen while I haul up first one and then the other suitcase onto the four-poster bed. Neutral themes abound, from the beige carpet and blinds, to the oversized bedspread in softly swirling shades of ivory, chocolate, and what looks like possibly a muted lilac.

I can hear Renata humming to herself while I hang up the seemingly endless array of clothing I brought for my stay. Hey, you never know what you're going to need. This is Hollywood, after all.

I am working on the second suitcase when Renata arrives in the doorway with my mimosa. I stop my work to accept the drink. I take a sip, eyes closed, savoring the flavor. "Yum."

"No doubt," Renata agrees. "What's the plan for while you're here? Although, if you want to sit on your ass the whole time, that would be fine, too."

I laugh at the thought. "Do you really think I could lounge around for a month or more without doing anything?"

"Nah, but I wanted to give you options."

"Gotcha. Thanks. Since I completely forgot to call her before I left, I plan to call Catherine tomorrow to see if she can arrange anything for me last minute. If not, I'll contact some agencies in the area and see what I can pick up on my own."

"Sounds like a plan. If Catherine doesn't have much, let me know. I can always contact my people and see if there are any photo shoots coming up that would be right for you."

"Hey, thanks." During our exchange, I have just about finished unpacking the last of my clothing. "I think I'll leave the toiletries for later. Let's go relax."

"Excellent suggestion," Renata comments and we head back to her living room, done in neutral shades similar to the guest bedroom. We take a seat on the voluminous chocolate-brown couch. "Sorry about the leather. I know you're not a fan."

I shrug. "It's your house. You can decorate it anyway you want," I reply as I lean back and sip at my mimosa.

And that was how my first day in LA went – relaxing with a friend.

CHAPTER TWENTY-FIVE

"Guess where I am?" I begin without preamble when Catherine answers her phone.

"Jail," comes her sardonic reply.

"Nice, but wrong. I'm in Los Angeles."

"Like I said, jail."

"Very funny."

"That's me. Why are you in Los Angeles?"

"I'm visiting with a friend of mine."

"When did this happen?" Catherine sounds confused.

"I flew out yesterday."

"Advance notice would have been nice."

"Hey," I reply defensively, "this was a last minute decision. Besides, I'm calling you now."

"How long will you be out there?"

"That remains to be seen. I'm calling to see what you can do for me out here. You know, in terms of pilot season or any other auditions, maybe."

There is a beat of silence before she answers. "I do know some people and I can certainly make some phone calls."

"That would be great."

"Let me do that now and I'll get back to you."

"Thanks, Catherine. You rock."

"Don't I know it," she responds before terminating the call. I turn to Renata with a smile on my face.

"Sounds like she should be able to help."

"I think so. Let's see what she can whip up from New York."

"Feel like coffee while you wait?"

"Sure – what's good around here?"

"Urth Caffe. You'll love it. C'mon," Renata says as she grabs her car keys.

"Sounds good to me," I respond and trail along behind her. After a quick drive up Beverly, we arrive at the coffee shop. "How'd you find this, instead of the usual Starbucks?" I ask as we take our place in line to order. It smells divine.

"A photographer friend recommended it. They're organic and even have a bunch of vegan products. Plus the desserts are exquisite."

"Really?" I can already hear my sweet tooth crying out for something delectable to go with the coffee. I've been studying the posted menu and at least know the drink I'm getting.

"Yes, but rich. You may not want to get one this early in the day." I raise an eyebrow at the statement. "Or maybe you would," she corrects herself with a laugh.

We place and collect our orders (I stick with just a cup of a drink called World Peace; how cool is that?), heading back outside to sit on the patio. We are continuing to chitchat when my cell phone rings from the depths of my purse.

"What's the word, Catherine?" I ask, again without preamble. Catherine is probably quite tired of my phone etiquette.

"How much do you love me?"

"More than I've ever loved anyone in my entire life."

"As well you should," she declares. "I've got you two auditions and a one-day shoot this week, plus I have a line on a few more things for the next couple of weeks."

"Excellent. You totally rock."

"Mmm, don't I know it," she concurs. "Tomorrow is the shoot. You'll be an under-five for a pilot re-shoot. Day after is an audition for a comedy pilot, possibly slated for ABC. And on Thursday, another audition for a vampire dramedy, along the lines of that show *The Vampire Diaries* that doesn't have network backing yet. It has a fairly famous lead already attached. Sound good?"

"Sounds awesome," I say enthusiastically and Renata smiles at my obvious excitement. Catherine gives me the details that I dutifully write down on a miniature pad of paper I keep in my purse for just this sort of occasion. I cap the pen when Catherine finishes.

"Any questions?"

"Nope. I'll let you know how they go – and call me if anything else gets firmed up."

"Of course. Ciao." Catherine terminates the call as I smile with satisfaction.

"So?" Renata asks. I detail everything Catherine just told me. "I'm glad she didn't find you anything for Friday."

"Oh yeah. Why?"

"You'll see."

"Ooh, a surprise. You know I don't like surprises."

"You always say that, but you lie. You totally dig surprises."

I shrug. "If you say so. I can wait until then to find out."

"Hah! The suspense will drive you batty. I'm not telling until at least Thursday evening. I want you to be able to dress appropriately."

"I appreciate the concern," I say solicitously.

"Of course, I look out for my girl."

"Dork." I throw my wadded up napkin at her and it bounces harmlessly off her shoulder.

Hey, I never said I was an athlete.

CHAPTER TWENTY-SIX

The morning of my first LA shoot dawns and I grab a doughnut to go with my coffee and take a seat at Renata's table.

"Here's your paper," she says, passing me the New York Post. I know, I know, I'm in Los Angeles. There's no reason for me to be reading the New York papers. But, it's like an addiction. I have to read the Page Six gossip. Just because I'm not there doesn't mean I want to be in the dark.

"Thanks." I skim through most sections and actually read the entertainment industry related sections (not just Page Six) while I scarf my doughnut and drink my joe. Interesting tidbits in the paper, but nothing too exciting. "What's your plan for today?"

"I'm working at the law firm today."

Soon I find myself buckling into her car and then she's slowly coming to a stop outside of a strip mall. "If you finish before 5 o'clock, you're on your own. Otherwise, call me on my cell when you're done and I'll swing by and get you."

"Thanks," I respond, opening the car door. "Have a good day at work, dear."

"You too, honey," she replies in a singsong voice.

I shut the car door and turn to face the store. Renata has dropped me off in front of, if you can believe it, a branch of a national chain furniture store. On either side of the large store are your standard strip mall accoutrements, like a beauty supply store and a locally owned dry cleaner. Catherine didn't have the details yesterday about the plot of this re-shooting pilot, but apparently, the location is a furniture store. Whatever.

Despite the sign on the door stating operating hours don't begin for another two hours, I push open the unlocked glass door and enter the establishment. Yep, this is the place. There are makeshift dividers, evident crew people scurrying around, and loads of filming equipment. I grab the first person who scurries close enough for me to reach.

"Hi, I'm a new cast member. Do you know where I go?"

The rather harried-looking individual stares at me for half a beat, making me wonder if I should repeat the question. "Yes. You need to see Vicki. She's in the back," he tells me, gesturing toward some of the makeshift dividers off to the right, deeper in the store. "She's responsible for talent."

"Great, thanks," I say, but he has already moved on to his next task. I head in the general direction he indicated, looking for someone new to ask as I get closer. Then I see a woman carrying a clipboard and wearing headphones. Yep, that's got to be Vicki.

"Excuse me, Vicki," I say, catching the redhead's attention. Curls swing in my direction as she snaps her head around to face me. "I'm Graciella Corsini. I'm in the cast," I add, since my name did not seem to trigger any sort of recognition.

"Yes?" Vicki's blue eyes flash and I can almost see her mind spinning, trying to place my name and person. The eyes refocus on me. "Right. The new girl."

I smile, with a bit of relief that I am, indeed, in the right place. "Yep, I'm the new girl."

"What have you been told about your part?"

"Just that it's an under-five."

"That's true, but you're in the background of nearly every scene." Yay! "I assume you can stay all day." This last stated rather than asked. She knows I wouldn't be there if I couldn't commit to all day. Whether LA or NYC – if I can't do it, they'll have someone new within the hour.

"Of course."

"Great." She looks me up and down, appraising, I'm assuming, my size. "Thank God they actually listened."

"Excuse me?"

"We have the wardrobe still from the original actress and we specifically requested that they send someone the same general size. They actually did it. It's a minor miracle." A response doesn't seem needed, so I remain quiet. "Okay, head over to wardrobe then," she points toward a glass-walled room where I can see now are many hanging items, "and get into the first outfit."

I begin to head in that direction when Vicki's hand on my arm stops me. "Wait." She rifles through some papers on her clipboard, finds what she's looking for, and hands a couple of pieces of paper to me. "Here's the breakdown for your stuff today, including your dialogue. That scene won't be until mid-afternoon, at the earliest. I assume you can have your few lines memorized by then." Again, a statement, not a question. Even with the dyslexia, I can handle four lines of dialogue.

"Of course," I instantly agree, taking the pages from her.

"Wonderful." And then she's off to her next piece of business and I resume walking toward the glass-walled room (maybe normally this is a showroom?)

"Hi, I'm the new Jessica," I inform the woman sitting in the room, sewing a button back onto a jacket. She gives me the same up and down appraisal that Vicki did and seems equally satisfied.

"Welcome to the set. I'm Laura. Your first outfit is a business casual pantsuit. You're one of the workers in the store, but remain in the background for the first day of the pilot. Okay?" She watches me expectantly.

"Okay."

"When we shoot the second day of the pilot this afternoon, you'll be a little more prominent and will wear a skirt and blouse combination. Okay?"

"Okay." Despite my penchant for talking, I actually like conversations like this where I have little to do except agree and make the other person happy. Things run much smoother that way.

Laura goes right to a particular section of the clothing and immediately finds what I naturally assume is my pantsuit for the morning. She hands the medium-gray pinstripe suit and lavender button-down blouse to me and directs me to a changing area.

"After you've changed into the wardrobe, head over to hair and makeup."

"Will do," I tell her and leave the glass-walled room with my suit.

Thirty minutes later, I am properly attired, with hair and makeup complete, awaiting the start of filming. There are five other individuals waiting with me. We introduce ourselves and chitchat until Vicki approaches us. She seems to be in charge of, well, everything.

"Everybody ready? Good. I want this stuff done before lunch."

And, just like that, we're off to the races. We spend the entire day re-shooting the comedy pilot. As best as I can tell, they actually rewrote half the script and replaced half the cast. It's meant to be a comedy, I think, but I can honestly say it'll be a miracle if any network picks up the show.

But, hey, it's a paycheck and I had fun.

After changing back into my own clothing and gathering what little belongings I brought on set, I head out of the furniture store and call Renata. It's only 5:30pm, so she should be home from work and we can still go grab dinner somewhere. A successful first day of work in Hollywood.

CHAPTER TWENTY-SEVEN

A few days later (after additional fabulous auditions) I'm reading the latest *People* magazine while I lounge on Renata's couch, waiting for her to finish primping. When at last she exits her bedroom, I can't quite control my mouth.

"Finally." I smile up at her, but don't actually move from my comfortable seat on the couch. "I assume you're going to a gig. Don't they have professionals for that?"

"Don't break my balls."

"What? *Don't break my balls?*" I snort laugh. "Now you're an Italian gangster?"

Renata grabs a pillow from the couch and swats at my head. I shriek and duck quickly enough that the pillow only whispers through my hair. I pick up the magazine that I dropped and walk to place it on the kitchen counter.

"That's right, missy. Don't make me have to put a cap in your ass."

I laugh, but wisely raise my hands in surrender, rather than continue to be a smart-ass.

Renata smiles and straightens up the couch cushions.

"Are we leaving now, Ms. Renata?" I say in a voice dripping with sugar and honey.

"Keep it up and you won't be going," Renata says warningly.

"I won't be going where? You still haven't told me what we're doing," I point out.

Renata glances at her watch before responding. "It's time to go find out." Without another word, she walks toward the door. You'd think I'd be a bigger fan of surprises, but I'm really not. I recognize, however, that more information will not be forthcoming, so, with a sigh, I follow Renata out to the car.

I don't even bother trying to figure out where we're headed as we drive. I fiddle with the radio instead and so it comes as kind of a shock when Renata pulls up to a security gate. A uniformed security guard approaches the driver's side window with a clipboard.

"Wow, he's official," I mumble sarcastically.

"Be good," Renata orders me before focusing her attention on the guard.

"Name," the security guard intones.

"Renata Harvey."

The guard reviews his list of individuals who may be permitted to have the green light to enter the hallowed grounds of... wait a minute, where are we? I crane my head around, looking for some sign. And, then I see it.

"Thank you, Ms. Harvey. You may drive through." The guard never even glances at Ms. Harvey's passenger.

"We're at the NBC studios!" I say with the excitement of a child finding a pony under the Christmas tree.

"No kidding," Renata responds and rolls her eyes at me. Mind you, I don't actually witness the eye rolling, but I can sense the eye rolling.

"Why are we here?" I ask and then remember, even as Renata is answering my question.

"I'm a Fallon girl and we're taping this afternoon."

"Sweet."

After parking the car and hiking for what seems like miles across a concrete desert, we arrive at the front doors of the NBC Studios in Burbank, California. I'm wondering if I'm going to meet Jimmy Fallon, when I realize Renata is talking to me.

"What?"

"Pay attention, Gracie."

"I am," I insist. "Now, anyway." I smile winningly and Renata chuckles.

"Normally, this is not a Take A Friend To Work kind of place, but I got permission from one of the segment producers to give you a tour."

"That's awesome, thanks."

"Keep in mind that you'll have to view the taping from the green room. You won't be able to actually be on the soundstage."

"Of course, no problem," I assure her.

"Let me do all the talking. Pretend you're mute."

I nod, without speaking, earning another eye roll. Her eyes are gonna get stuck in the back of her head if she keeps doing that.

"Let's go," Renata says, pulling open one side of large glass double doors.

The lobby is unpretentious, but clearly entertainment-related, with flat screen televisions dotting the walls, displaying various NBC shows for a waiting guest's viewing pleasure. Renata heads toward an attractive young woman sitting behind a large desk. The woman smiles at our approach.

"Can I help you?"

"Renata Harvey, here for the Fallon taping."

A few keystrokes at the computer later and the receptionist ushers us into the inner sanctum. Renata and I walk through open wooden doors and go left down a carpeted hallway, replete with photos of famous people, dead and alive. We arrive at a bank of elevators and instead of stopping, as I expect, Renata continues to a small stairwell. I follow her down one flight of stairs, silently marveling at the apparent emptiness thus far of the building. Exiting the stairwell at the bottom of the stairs, we walk into chaos.

People are milling around everywhere, some walking with purpose, others truly milling, as though with no final destination in mind. The volume is high, though not painful.

"C'mon," Renata says, grabbing my hand and pulling me past people, down another short hallway, to an open door.

There are two women already in the room when we enter and they turn to greet us.

"Hey, Renata," a redhead in jeans and a tank top says from her perch on a stool at a row of mirrors to our left. "You must be Gracie," she addresses me. "I'm Roxie." Before I can do more than smile and nod, the blond reading a magazine on the couch against the back wall offers her greeting as well.

"Hi, guys. Gracie, I'm Denise," she directs this last toward me.

"It's nice to meet you both," I respond and take a seat on the couch with the blond. Renata sits on a stool opposite Roxie the redhead and swivels to smile at me.

"Welcome to the world of late night television."

"What happens now?" I ask the women in the room.

"The three of us will get our hair and makeup done in," Renata consults her watch, "about 30 minutes. Shooting will begin about 30 minutes after that. Our bit is at the beginning. You can watch it on that television," Renata indicates a small television set I overlooked in the corner. "It's hooked into the in-house feed, so you can watch the taping," she explains before I can ask. "After we're through, I'll come grab you and give you a quick – quiet – tour of the set and offices I'm familiar with. Sound good?"

"Sounds great."

Renata, Denise, Roxie, and I shoot the breeze for the next 25 minutes until a production assistant sticks his head in the doorway to inform the ladies it's time.

"Have fun," I call out as they exit the room.

Renata, bringing up the rear, gives me a knowing smile. "Be good."

"Always," I reply, with an angelic smile.

After Renata follows her friends out of the room, I briefly contemplate exploring the set furtively without her. My Bad Angel puts up a good fight, but in the end, my Good Angel wins by reminding me that this is Renata's job and I could get her in trouble if I begin randomly wandering. I'm such a good friend.

I compromise with myself by standing in the doorway, so I can at least watch the activity. I'm evidently enthralled enough that I don't immediately notice the flickering light on the television screen. When I finally do, it's apparent that Fallon is well into his opening monologue. I cross the room to turn up the volume on the set and settle in on the couch to watch the taping.

I'm probably biased, but when they get to the bit featuring Renata and the other girls, Renata totally steals the scene. The women don't have any lines of dialogue – they basically bring props onto the stage – but Renata's mere presence is luminous. I spontaneously clap when she exits the shot.

"That was awesome," I tell Renata when she reappears in the flesh and enters the room.

"You're sweet, but please. It's a glorified extra part and you know it. Fun, though," she acknowledges.

"And it's a recurrent part on a national television show," I remind her.

"True," she concedes. "Enough about that. Are you ready for your tour?"

"Absolutely."

"I know you're not an entertainment newbie, but remember to be quiet."

"I know, I know. You don't have to worry about me," I assure her. "I'll contain my enthusiasm."

And so we begin our silent tour, with Renata whispering and miming (you know, like a mime) information to me, with me trying not to laugh out loud at her antics. Renata points out the green rooms for the other guests (Chris Hemsworth for that taping – nice) and the set equivalent of the wings of a theatrical stage, before bringing me upstairs to show me the production offices, including the segment producers, the talent bookers, and the writers. Naturally, it is like a ghost town because of the taping, but it is cool to imagine the everyday hustle and bustle of a late night television show.

After the tour, Renata and I return to her green room to watch the remainder of the taping. Roxie and Denise apparently cleared out after they were finished, as there remains no evidence of their presence in the room. By the time the show finishes, Renata has changed back into her street clothes.

"Are we ready to go?"

"Almost," Renata responds. Having gathered her belongings, she elaborates. "We have one stop to make before we leave."

I nod my understanding and follow Renata from the room. Instead of heading for the stairs to return to the ground floor, Renata leads me to the elevators, one of which we take back up to the production offices.

Stepping off the elevator, I see the back of a man shaking hands with another man who looks vaguely familiar. Tim Cleary, I suddenly recall from my tour earlier. He is a segment producer and was one of the only production staff actually in his office during the earlier tour.

Mr. Cleary says a final goodbye and disappears behind a door as his companion turns to the reception desk. He grabs a piece of paper off of the desk and is writing a note about something while we cross the room toward him. My Spidey senses begin tingling as I study the profile of the man.

"Is that Zac Efron?" I ask quietly, mouth agape.

Renata smiles enigmatically and answers my question with, "Let me introduce you." She turns to the unbelievably attractive man now standing a mere two feet away. "David?" He turns from the desk and smiles when he sees Renata. "This is my friend Gracie."

"Hey, David," I manage to sputter as we shake hands.

"It's nice to meet you," he responds, in a voice quite familiar. Hmm, he looks and sounds exactly like Zac Efron, but Renata called him David. Is this some elaborate joke at my expense?

"Are we still on for tonight?" Renata asks.

"Naturally," David replies.

"What's tonight?" I ask.

"You didn't tell her," David teases Renata.

"I thought it'd be a nice surprise." Did I say I didn't like surprises? I've completely changed my mind.

David glances at his watch. "What do you say we meet up in a few hours for dinner? 8 o'clock?"

"Are you still thinking Osteria?"

"I think your friend will like it," David says and gives me a look that melts my insides. Oh, those beautiful blue eyes.

"See you at 8, then," Renata confirms. I simply smile and nod, having apparently been robbed of the power of speech by lust.

Clearly not finished with whatever he was writing, David remains at the desk as Renata and I walk back to the elevators. I manage to remain silent until the second the elevator doors close behind us.

I spin to face Renata. "So?"

"So, what?"

"Don't be dense. Was that him?"

"Who?"

"Zac Efron, that's who?"

Renata pauses for a beat. "Does it matter?"

"Of course it does," I immediately respond and then pause for a beat of my own to reconsider. Renata remains silent as I recall my initial thoughts upon meeting David. As we step off the elevator on the ground floor, I shrug.

"Nah, it doesn't matter in the least."

"Glad to hear it," Renata says with a laugh.

CHAPTER TWENTY-EIGHT

Renata and I arrive back at her house and spend an interminable amount of time preparing for our fab evening out, eventually arriving only fifteen minutes late at Osteria Mozza. Luckily, traffic on Melrose Avenue was relatively light, or we would have been much later.

"There he is," Renata says as we approach the restaurant. Sure enough, David stands outside the door awaiting our arrival. As if sensing he's being talked and thought about, he glances in our direction. He lifts a hand in greeting and smiles.

"Hey, David," I say as we reach him. Some men are just too beautiful for words.

He looks, well, dapper is the best way to describe it. He could have stepped out of the 30s or 40s in his attire. Hmm, in fact, he looks much like Zac Efron does in *Me and Orson Welles*. Oh well, no use taking that thought any further.

David is wearing a black patterned vest over a crisp white tailored shirt, with trousers and loafers. The outfit screams sophisticated classic. Although, I suppose, screaming would be too gauche.

"It's good to see you again, Gracie," David replies with another smile. My God, his face lights up when he smiles. Okay, stop it, I instruct myself. I can't keep gushing whenever he does, well, anything. I'll be exhausted by the end of the night.

"You, too, David."

"You both look outstanding."

I should hope so given the length of time we spent prepping. Even being objective, I have to admit that Renata and I are rocking our outfits. We're wearing cocktail dresses with 4-inch strappy sandals. Renata's dress is maroon, with spaghetti straps, a fitted bodice, and a slinky bottom ending several inches above her knees. The dress is a shiny but silky fabric and a lesser woman might look like a tramp, but with her upswept do and regal features, Renata is nothing but class. My dress, though equally short, is a deep emerald shift with a halter neckline that gracefully skims my body. We opted for no jewelry and minimal makeup.

David gives Renata a quick hug then opens the restaurant door. "After you, ladies."

Mmm, how I love the smell of Italian food. We enter into what I surmise to be the main dining area, as there appears to also be an area leading to outdoor seating, as well as stairs to a (probably) private dining area above. Not that we'd be able to easily get to any of that, mind you. Apparently, 8 o'clock is the magic dining hour today in Los Angeles, based on the crowd of people waiting to be seated. Renata and I follow David to the host (*maitre d'* maybe?) to put our names on the wait list.

But, *au contraire, mon amies*. The host taking names and checking reservations is as captivated by David as the waiting patrons are.

Renata leans over to whisper in my ear. "Normally, you need to make reservations about a month in advance."

"Dang, really?"

Renata nods.

I can't hear what David says over the din of the restaurant, but after he leans in and speaks softly to the host, we are immediately seated. Renata smiles broadly at me. The benefits of dining with Zac Efron... or his look-a-like.

The three in our dining party follow another member of the Osteria Mozza staff past an amazing mozzarella bar (surrounded by what look like marble stands, no less) to a semi-secluded table. Our drink orders are quickly taken and we are left to peruse the menu.

"That is an amazing wine rack," I comment, as I crane my head around in an attempt to determine its full size.

"Yes, it is," David agrees. "It envelops the entire dining room."

Renata laughs at this comment.

"What?" David asks.

"You sound like a restaurant guide review."

I laugh with Renata, while David, with a slight shake of his head, merely smiles.

"Can I help it if I'm a fan?"

"Not at all," Renata allows.

"If the food is as good as the decor, I'll probably be an even bigger fan," I chime in.

"Thank you, Gracie."

"Suck up," Renata helpfully adds. I stick my tongue out at her and David laughs aloud.

"Very mature, Gracie."

"Who lied and told you I was mature, Renata?" My standard line, but we both laugh.

"Ladies, ladies. Maybe we should take a look at the menu?"

"That sounds good," I say between chuckles.

Since we ordered water to drink and turned down the wine list (why get overpriced alcohol here when we're just gonna get overpriced alcohol somewhere else later?), we focus our attention on the mozzarella bar and entree options.

"What are you guys getting?" Renata asks.

"Is there anything vegetarian that you would recommend?" I ask David by way of reply.

"You're a vegetarian?" When I nod, David studies the menu for a moment, then answers my question. "The gnocchi is excellent. That one would be a good first choice."

"Works for me," I agree and place my menu at the corner of the table. "Thanks."

"Of course. Oh, and I'm having the tortellini," David informs Renata in answer to her earlier question. She nods and bites her lower lip as she continues to study the menu.

The waiter arrives at that moment to take our order.

"We'll start with the burrata from Basilicata," David begins. At my inquisitive look, he adds, "Trust me, you'll love it."

"Okay," I agree. The waiter looks to me for my dinner order. "I'll have the gnocchi al pomodoro."

"And for you, ma'am?"

"David, why don't you order?"

"Do you need another minute, Renata?" David asks.

"Nah, I'm fine," she replies. "Just do your order first."

"Of course. I'll have the tortellini."

The waiter returns his attention to Renata, who puts the menu aside with a sigh. "I'll have the maccharoni."

"Very good," intones the waiter before departing.

"What are we doing after dinner?" I ask.

"Don't worry about it," is Renata's reply.

"Oh, c'mon. Just a tiny hint."

"We're going out."

"Thanks, David, that was helpful," I respond dryly.

No amount of wheedling on my part results in any additional disclosures from my companions. Soon the mozzarella bar order arrives and I am too distracted to continue pressing for more information.

"David, you were right," I tell him between mouthfuls. "This cheese is divine."

"I'm glad I chose well."

"Indeed," Renata says.

As though being watched by the uber-attentive wait staff, our entrees arrive not more than thirty seconds after we finish the delightful burrata appetizer. And, of course, they are perfection. When we finish our last bites, the waiter materializes and offers the dessert menu. Although stuffed, we decide to split an order of cioccolato. That's a bittersweet chocolate cake with perugian chocolates, I found out.

"I have died and gone to heaven," Renata says after her first bite of the dessert.

"No kidding," I concur. "This is delicious."

"I guess you ladies really like your chocolate," David says with a smirk. We pointedly ignore him and the three of us continue eating the cake.

"That was possibly one of the best desserts I've ever had," Renata declares as the last bite is eaten.

"I'm glad you enjoyed it so much," David says.

"The whole dinner was amazing," I cannot help but gush (again) at David.

"I knew you would like it, Gracie," David tells me, giving me another one of those looks that melts my insides. Yep, still melting. We break eye contact and David checks his watch. "Almost perfect timing."

"You mean for us to do the secret next part of the fab evening?" I ask teasingly.

"Yes, exactly," David deadpans.

I look back and forth between David and Renata. "I can't believe you guys were able to keep this a secret. Although soon

I'll find out," I say excitedly, actually clapping my hands in childlike delight. Guess maybe I do like surprises.

The waiter arrives then to hand David the check.

"Don't even think about it," David tells us, although in truth neither Renata nor I had even begun making a move toward our wallets. He's such a gentleman.

The waiter quickly retrieves the bill and David's credit card. Just as the waiter walks away, I realize I missed a golden opportunity to confirm or disconfirm David as Zac Efron. I just need to get a glimpse of the name on his credit card when the waiter returns.

Unfortunately, David seems to sense my thoughts through some psychic connection, because he manages to carefully retrieve his credit card and return it to its home in his billfold without enabling me even the smallest of glimpses.

"Are we ready, ladies?"

"I don't know, since I don't know what we're doing."

"Hush up, Gracie. Actually David, we're gonna need a few minutes when we're back at the car."

"Of course. It's only 11:15pm anyway."

"We are?"

"Yes, Gracie."

The three of us traipse back to the car (a rental, I realize now) and Renata heads immediately for the rear.

"Pop the trunk." Seconds later, the trunk unlocks and slowly rises upward. Inside is a backpack I don't remember seeing Renata place in the trunk at all.

"What's that?"

"A backpack."

"No shit, smart ass. Whatcha got in there? Are we going camping?"

"Ha ha, funny girl," Renata replies as she reaches in to retrieve the backpack. From within its depths, she removes long beaded necklaces that just happen to complement our dresses perfectly – they even evoke a 20s flapper feel. Hey, I'm sensing a theme here, as I glance over at David's retro outfit. After Renata and I don the necklaces, she next withdraws two sets of sparkly drop earrings.

"Fancy vintage jewelry? Wherever could we be going?" I feign an air of sudden knowledge brought about by the jewelry.

"Please. You have no idea where we're going," Renata counters, seeing through my feigned epiphany.

"Okay, no, I don't."

"You'll know soon enough," she reminds me as she hauls out her portable makeup case. "Now, sit still and shut up."

I comply and Renata expertly applies my makeup.

"You have some serious talent in this department," I tell Renata while I admire her handiwork in a compact mirror and she effects her own transformation.

David, who has been waiting in the car listening to the radio, opens the door when he hears the trunk slam shut.

"May I see?"

"Of course, darling," La Renata replies. I know we look smashing the instant I see David's reaction.

"I didn't think either of you could be more beautiful," he says flirtatiously.

"Aren't you sweet?" I respond with a honeyed tone. The intensity when our gazes lock causes my smile to falter slightly and my cheeks to flush.

"Okay," I say, sounding fluttery to my own ears. "Let's go to this secret place I've heard nothing about."

David smiles brilliantly at us both. "Ladies, your chariot awaits."

After we pile back into the car, David flies us through Los Angeles in our winged chariot. Okay, maybe not literally, but it was a nice ride. The car was some foreign sedan whose make I didn't catch. Anyway, David begins to slow when we turn onto Ivar Avenue, a fairly unlit street I've never heard of.

"Where are we going?" I can't help but ask. "What could possibly be on this tiny street?"

"Quit asking, Gracie," Renata says without rancor, despite the fact that I've asked this question incessantly.

"Okay, okay, sorry. Inquiring minds want to know." Lights are appearing brighter as we travel down the street. "We're going to the Cabana Club," I state rather than ask as we pull up to the valet.

"No, we're not," David responds. "The place we're going to shares a valet service with the Cabana Club."

"Besides, the Cabana Club is a meat market," Renata explains.

"Why don't we want to go there?" I ask with a laugh. Neither bothers to respond, but I can see David smiling in the rearview mirror.

David hands his car keys to the valet and our trio makes its way to the nondescript green door marking the entrance to our destination. Of course, at first the door was invisible, owing to the easily ten people deep crowd around it. Amazingly, the crowd parts for us, as though by magic, and soon we are standing at the door.

"We don't have a reservation," David tells the man who holds the keys to the kingdom – or at least the guest list.

"Normally, without a reservation on a Friday night, there's no way you or I are getting in," Renata whispers in my ear.

"No problem, sir," the man with the guest list says. Just like at Osteria Mozza. Must be nice to have the world open before you. "How many are in your party?"

"Three."

"Welcome to the Green Door." Entering the Green Door is like stepping back in time to a party held at a turn-of-the-century

French estate. There are red velvet couches, iron tables, and portraits that look like they could be of actual dead royalty. Oh, and chandeliers. At a nightclub.

David leads us through a rather classy-looking crowd to seats at one of the two bars.

"What'll you have?"

David defers to us to order from the bartender first.

"How close can you get to a blackberry martini?" I had one once when visiting San Francisco and am hoping I might get lucky since I'm on the west coast again.

"Pretty close," the bartender answers with a smile.

"I'll have the driest martini you can make," Renata requests.

"And for you, sir?"

"I'll try one of those blackberry martinis," David orders with a glance at me. "They sound intriguing."

"You won't be disappointed," I assure him as the bartender departs to make our drinks.

"I'm sure not," David responds meaningfully. Double entendre? I think so. I hope so?

With a suggestive smile, I give a slight shake of my head. I turn to survey the room's inhabitants. It is an interesting mix of 20-somethings and up, all dressed to impress. I face the bar again when our drinks are prepared. David slides a large bill across the bar.

"Keep the change." The bartender nods his acknowledgement. The three of us retrieve our martinis and take delicate sips.

"Wow, he did get it pretty close," I say.

"I don't know what the original tasted like, but this is quite good," David agrees.

"Not bad," Renata adds as we look to her for comment.

"Now that we have our libations, it's time for a change of scenery," David declares.

"Lead the way," I consent, holding my drink aloft.

Renata and I trail David as he traverses the club, past an open-air stone lounge where people are eating and along a hallway that snakes around the side of the building. We stop at a cozy nook and crowd together on one of the red velvet couches. The room seems filled to capacity with your stereotypical Hollywood crowd.

"Hey, isn't that Paris Hilton?" I ask as I glimpse the stick-thin blond dilettante.

"I thought they were more exclusive than that," Renata comments archly. David and I laugh. "That's more like it," she continues, having eyed someone better on the other side of the room.

"Who?" I ask, trying to see whom she sees. And then I do. "Oh, yeah. Nice."

Now David is curious whom we're talking about. "Who is it?"

"I don't remember his name, but he's on one of those *CSI* shows," I answer.

"Excuse me friends. I'm off to make an introduction."

"Have fun. Be safe," I respond. Renata gives us her *I'm about to be naughty* look and saunters toward the actor. David and I watch the obviously interested reaction when Renata reaches her destination.

"Guess you're stuck with me for the night," David says with a smile.

I feign disappointment. "Yeah. That's too bad. I may have to trade up later."

"Ouch," David replies, touching my arm companionably. I swear I can feel the spark between us as our eyes meet and I gulp down the remainder of my martini.

David arches an eyebrow. "Would you like another?"

"Are you trying to get me drunk?"

"Do I need to?"

"Not in the least."

David attracts the attention of a waitress and orders two more martinis. As we drink several (who knows how many?) rounds, I occasionally glance at Renata and the actor.

"Hey, they left," I say, when the spot where they had been in filled with new people.

After visually confirming my statement, David glances at his watch. "It's almost 2am. That's closing time." Somehow we had missed a bartender's shout of last call, although maybe the Green Door is too classy for shouting that sort of thing.

"That's when I turn into a pumpkin," I comment tipsily.

"Really? I thought it was midnight."

"Damn." I squint at him, evidently in deep thought while my alcohol-soaked brain processes the comment. "I guess I'm already a pumpkin."

"Funny, you don't look like a pumpkin. And, unless I'm remembering my fairytale incorrectly, I thought it was the carriage that turned into a pumpkin."

I sigh dramatically. "You're probably right. Maybe we should check on your car," I suggest with a laugh.

"We certainly could, although I suspect it's snug in its valet slot."

"Prolly," I agree. My eyes narrow suspiciously. "Why aren't you drunk?"

"Who says I'm not?"

"You're far too logical and," here I stop, as I lose my train of thought.

"And?" David prompts.

"I don't know. The thought is gone," I say with a wave of my hand. "You know," I continue as I cuddle next to David on the couch, "we could still go check on the car. After all, it's nearly closing time." I feel David's arm tighten around me.

"Yes, we could," he whispers in my ear. Together we rise from the couch and I am mildly surprised that I don't really need assistance. David waves to a handful of people as we exit the club. Our car magically appears, courtesy of the valet, and I sink into the front seat.

"I like the view better from up here," I announce after David has taken his seat behind the wheel. "Hey, I get it," I say suddenly.

"Get what?" I can hear amusement in his voice.

"You didn't drink much because you knew you had to drive us home." I am proud of how smart I am, figuring that out, despite the alcohol.

David places his hand on my knee and I shift in his direction like a plant toward sunlight. "You are absolutely correct. I thought I'd impress you with my responsible nature."

"Honey, everything about you impresses me," I tell him and his hand massages higher on my thigh.

"What do you want to do?" He has pulled away from the clubs and is driving down the street.

I am all set to suggest *anywhere we can get naked* when, even through my alcohol-soaked brain, I realize this is a mistake. Drinking and sexing (is that a real word?) out in LA isn't going to make me forget the pain caused by my uncertain relationship with Julian. An image of Julian's smile comes unbidden to my mind and I sigh sadly.

"What is it?" David can sense the change in my mood and is confused, but removes his hand from my thigh.

"I think you need to take me home."

"Of course. Is everything okay?" He sounds genuinely concerned for me.

"No, it's not," I say and then am mortified as I begin to cry. David immediately pulls into a parking lot.

"Gracie, please tell me what's wrong."

"It's a long, tortured story," I warn him dramatically and when he doesn't change his mind about knowing, I proceed to describe my instant connection with Julian, the unfortunate fact of Julian's marriage, and how I fled to LA to escape the pain.

"Gracie, I'm so sorry," David offers.

"Thanks." I sniffle slightly as the tears finish. "Thanks for listening."

"You're welcome," David says with a smile. "Are you ready to return to Renata's?"

I simply nod and David eases the car out onto the road. A short time later, we arrive at Renata's. Turning off the car, David walks around to open my door. He holds out his hand in invitation.

"My lady."

I take his hand, allowing him to help me from the car. After I alight from the vehicle, we walk arm-in-arm to the door.

"Thank you for a lovely evening, Gracie."

"Thank you, too, David. I'm sorry I was such a spazz."

"Don't even think about it. Probably for the best, anyway, all things considered."

"Yeah, you're probably right."

David gives me a chaste kiss on the cheek and waits for me to unlock and open the front door. I see the hallway light is on and know that Renata got home safely.

"Good night, Gracie," David says as I start to cross the threshold. "Gracie?"

I stop and turn toward him. "Yes?"

"Do you really want to know if I'm Zac Efron?"

I smile. "I would love to know."

David leans over and whispers his identity in my ear. And the answer is…a lady never tells.

CHAPTER TWENTY-NINE

The next month passes in the same fashion. Filming the two jobs I land from my first week of auditions (and unsuccessfully auditioning for more, but we'll ignore that) and hanging with the A-list celebs courtesy of Renata. And then my new world gets blown apart when I open the New York Post (that, yes, I have continued to read even after a month in LA because, well, I'm a New Yorker, born and bred.) My shit followed me to LA.

"That's an interesting development," I say into the silence at breakfast with Renata in her kitchen.

Renata looks at me quizzically.

"Did you read Page Six – you know, the gossip column?"

"You know I don't read that sophomoric nonsense."

I roll my eyes. "Well, there's an interesting item about a certain soap opera star."

"Do tell. I'm intrigued."

"Nah, you said you don't care for – what did you call it? – sophomoric nonsense. I'll save your delicate sensibilities."

"Shut up and tell me," Renata orders, without rancor.

"Julian filed for divorce."

Renata's eyebrows shoot up. "Ooh, that is interesting."

"I know."

"Have you talked to him?"

I shake my head. "Not since I moved out here."

"Will you talk to him now?"

I shake my head again in the negative.

"Why not?"

"One, I don't know if this is true," I point out. "It's a gossip column item."

"True," Renata acknowledges.

"Two, I don't know the circumstances of the divorce."

"So?"

"I left the ball in his court, so to speak, when I left. This doesn't change that."

"What? You know I don't do sports metaphors."

"Smart ass."

"Seriously, who cares how you left it? If he's single again, you should call him."

I shrug noncommittally. "Maybe if I get confirmation of the divorce."

"You aren't going to call him," Renata says with certainty.

"You think you know me that well?" Renata says nothing and I smile. She knows me so well.

CHAPTER THIRTY

They say that when it rains it pours. No – waiting for the other shoe to drop is a more apropos expression. I should have heard the other shoe dropping when my cell phone rang a mere day after my breakfast conversation with Renata about Julian. The number seemed vaguely familiar and I answered the call with a question in my voice. "Hello?"

"Graciella Corsini?" Oh no, I recognize that voice. "It's Aliana Gregson, with the district attorney's office."

"Hi, how are you?" I ask with a fake concern worthy of a Southern belle.

"I'm doing well. I'm sorry to bother you," Ms. Gregson says without preamble, "but I have information you should hear."

Great, I think with trepidation. Her tone of voice is reserved for news of death, or impending death. I wonder which this is.

"Assistant District Attorney Leonard Myers was found dead yesterday," she informs me bluntly.

"What?" I ask, more to let her know that I heard her than because I missed any part of that succinct but informative sentence.

"He was murdered," Ms. Gregson continues, pausing for my reaction. I do not disappoint.

"Oh, God. Why?" My mind is racing. Did this have anything to do with the case against Tommy?

"We don't know. We don't have any reason to believe that his death was connected to the Thomas Pullman case," she hurries to add, as if reading my mind.

"Then why are you calling me?" I ask, though I already know the answer.

"Just as a precautionary measure," she insists. "I really want to stress that we do not believe you are in any danger."

"Better safe than sorry," I reply woodenly.

"Well, yes."

"Was there anything else?"

"No. Gracie, I'm sorry this got brought up again. Please try to remember that ADA Myers put a lot of bad people behind bars. Any one of them could be responsible."

"Plus, Tommy's case was dismissed," I say hopefully.

"Exactly. That's why this truly is a precautionary measure and in no way indicative of the level of the threat to you personally."

Despite the earlier news, I laugh. "You sounded so much like a lawyer right then."

Ms. Gregson chuckles. "Occupational hazard."

"I'm sure."

"I'll call you if anything else develops."

"Thanks."

We say our goodbyes and I close the phone. I lean back on Renata's couch, close my eyes, and promptly fall asleep. My next moment of awareness is Renata's voice piercing the quiet.

"Hey girl, I'm home," I hear from the distance of the foyer and a layer of sleep. I mumble something she undoubtedly cannot hear from her location.

"Are you sleeping?" This time she sounds louder, as she must have entered the living room and I am practically awake. My eyes flutter open.

"I was," I yawn. "What time is it?"

"Just after six," she answers without checking. She's probably right.

"I can't believe I fell asleep."

"Are you still up for dinner tonight?"

"Definitely. Especially since I'm going back to New York next week."

Renata doesn't look surprised. "Good for you."

"That's not why I'm going back." I tell her about Aliana Gregson's phone call.

"Why would you go back, if you just found out that this attorney was killed? Isn't that like jumping into the fire?" Renata sounds genuinely worried.

"Kinda," I concede. "My logic," if it can be called that, "is that if the murder was indeed connected, which nobody thinks it is, I can keep an eye on my family, and Jane."

"Why Jane?"

"It's always the roommate of the target who ends up accidentally dead."

Renata laughs. "That is some stretched logic, but you know I support you."

"Thanks."

"I still think it's the other thing."

I smile mischievously. "Maybe partly."

"I knew it."

"No need to gloat."

"It's cool. Where do you want to go to dinner?"

CHAPTER THIRTY-ONE

"Hey, mama," I begin the phone call in a cheerful voice.

"What's wrong?"

"Why would anything be wrong? I just called to tell you I'm coming back to New York next week," I hurry to add. My attempt to distract my mother is successful.

"That's wonderful, Graciella," she exclaims. "We have missed you."

"I've missed you, too."

"You will come over Saturday for dinner," she informs me.

"I wouldn't miss it," I assure her. "You'll make sure everybody's there?"

"You insult me," she says with mock indignation and I laugh.

"I apologize, mama."

"Apology accepted." I can hear the smile in her voice and decide not to tell her the reason I'm coming home.

"I've got to go, but I'll call you when I have my flight information." I've almost gotten out of telling her. We just have to say goodbye.

"Why come back now?"

So close. Like a laser sight, she refocuses her attention. Do I tell her that the attorney from my case is dead? Or do I tell a partial truth and tell her that my married almost-lover filed for divorce? Potential future son-in-law definitely trumps possible death.

"Do you remember Julian McNamara?"

"Yes," she replies succinctly and I swear I can almost hear her cross herself.

"He's filed for divorce from his wife."

"Now you can have him?" My mother's question floors me.

"What?"

"He is available now, yes?"

"Yes, I suppose."

"Then you can have him."

"He's going to be divorced," I remind my Roman-Catholic mother.

"Do you love him?"

I sigh. "Yes," I finally admit.

"That is all that matters."

"What about papa?"

"I handle your father."

I suddenly realize my eyes are welling up. I blink back the tears. "Thanks, mama."

"I love you, Graciella."

"I love you, too, mama."

Now we say our goodbyes, but I'm barely listening as I ponder the conversation. I'm so glad I wasn't completely successful at evading her questions.

After I compose myself, I make similar, though less weepy and more disclosing, phone calls to my agent and my roommate, to inform them of my plans. Catherine and I arrange lunch for after I return. Jane is not as alarmed about the attorney's death as I had thought she would be.

Unusual how often people have been surprising me lately.

The next week I can barely sleep the night before my flight. I feel like a kid at Christmas, only the gift is so much greater than a dollhouse could ever be. I'm going home.

EAST COAST, REVISITED

CHAPTER THIRTY-TWO

Ahh. The East Coast. What was I thinking? I'm a Manhattanite through and through. I'm on my way to meet Catherine for lunch. The move back to the city was completely uneventful and Jane was happy to have my company in the apartment again. And Catherine had told me she had good news for me…I can hardly wait to hear what it is.

I open the door to Caravan of Dreams, a great vegetarian restaurant in the East Village, and spot Catherine sitting at a table. I half gesture at the table when I see a server look like she's about to come greet me and then I walk over to Catherine.

"Welcome home, Gracie," Catherine greets me while we hug hello.

"Thanks Catherine," I reply as we take our seats. "It's great to be back. I love LA, but New York is home."

"Of course it is. And New York missed you."

"Oh, yeah?"

"Before I get to that, congratulations again on your success while you were in Los Angeles."

"Well, it was mixed success, but thanks. And thanks for arranging the auditions."

"You're welcome."

The waitress appears and we order our standard drinks and dishes. We resume our conversation when the waitress departs.

"I had a blast on those projects. Hanging out with my friend and her celebrity pals was a riot."

"I can only imagine. Let's get down to business. Not that I don't enjoy your company, of course," she adds with a smile. "I have good news I'm sure you're going to want to hear."

"Tell me, tell me," I urge her, with excitement.

"*Heart's Home* called." Here she pauses for dramatic effect.

"Yes?" I pretend beg, playing her game.

"They want you back next week for a guest spot for your TV brother's wedding."

"Cool."

"There's more."

I wait, not quite with bated breath, but with no small measure of interest.

"They want you for a guest spot as a prelude to bringing you in as a regular contract player." Catherine looks like she's about to pop. I can barely believe what I'm hearing and am simply speechless.

"What do you think? Oh, and before you worry about it, they're perfectly willing to accommodate your," here she lowers her voice, "dyslexia, if you accept."

I'm grinning widely now. "Accept? Wild dogs couldn't keep me away."

Catherine wrinkles her nose. "Wild dogs?"

"Never mind," I laugh. "Of course I accept."

"Excellent."

"What day is it? When do I get the first script?"

"Relax, Gracie. I'll give you all the pertinent details."

I take a deep breath and by the time we finish lunch, I do indeed have all the details. Believe it or not, it's not until I'm heading for the subway station, when I realize what else this fabulous opportunity means. Weddings on a daytime drama involve most of the show's cast and Julian will certainly be present. I stop so suddenly that the pedestrian behind me nearly collides with me. He shoots me a look as he walks around, but I am oblivious.

Oh my. I'm going to see Julian.

Physically shaking my head to clear those thoughts, I resume walking. Of course, my mind is flooded with imagined glances and conversations on set with Julian. By the time I reach home, I am mentally exhausted. Jane is at work, having gone in early for the dinner shift at the restaurant today, and I have the apartment to myself. Seeing today's paper on the coffee table, I decide to distract myself with other people's news.

"Good grief," I say to the empty apartment after I read the local section front-page headline. "I really should just stop reading the paper."

Mob Associate Arrested For Murder the headline screams, but that isn't what has rattled me. After all, mob guys get arrested for murder fairly regularly. No, what have me rattled are the pictures of the mob associate and his victim. Creepy Guy with the seersucker suit and ADA Myers. Tommy's associate, whose given name is apparently Nicholas Rossini, shot Leonard Myers execution-style. Before I fully realize I am doing so, my fingers are dialing on my cell phone.

"Ms. Gregson, this is Gracie Corsini."

"Hello, Gracie. What can I do for you?"

"Have you seen the paper today?" I answer a question with a question.

She immediately understands, or thinks she does, anyway. "We arrested Leonard's killer. He's in organized crime, but that doesn't mean he's necessarily connected to Thomas Pullman, or your case."

"You don't understand," I insist, hearing a tinge of hysteria in my voice. "I know him."

"Right, ADA Myers," Ms. Gregson says patiently.

"No, the other one. Rossini."

"You do?" Her voice takes on an edge.

"He's the creepy guy I could never fully describe, who was with Tommy when I was threatened."

"I can understand why you would be concerned," she says.

"Can you? Tommy and Rossini threatened me, then the prosecutor from Tommy's case just happens to be killed, and now Rossini's out on bond."

"I realize this is difficult, but please try to remain calm and think it through logically. Why would Pullman or Rossini risk drawing attention to themselves by hurting people associated with a dismissed case? This murder is almost certainly unrelated to your case and related to any number of organized crime cases that Leonard worked on."

I take a few deep breaths and recognize that she's probably right. Probably. "Because he's crazy," I can't help but respond, though my voice does sound considerably less hysterical.

Perhaps sensing I have calmed down, Ms. Gregson chuckles. "That's likely true, but he's always demonstrated enough common sense to evade jail."

"Good point," I concede.

"Just keep me informed on the off chance we're wrong and you see something that worries you."

"I will, thank you." I find that I do feel calmer. We say our goodbyes and I continue to read the paper, skipping every story about murder. Why continue to invite stress in?

CHAPTER THIRTY-THREE

"Hey George," I greet the portly security guard.

"Gracie? Hi! Welcome back," he responds enthusiastically.

"Thanks. It's great to be back." I place my backpack on the conveyor belt and walk through the metal detector. When it doesn't beep, George waves me through. I collect my backpack off the conveyor belt and walk to the reception desk.

"Go on in, Ms. Corsini," the receptionist says before I can re-introduce myself. "You're in the same dressing room as before."

I thank her and walk through the double doors, down a series of hallways until I arrive at the dressing room I previously shared with Danielle, Kris, and Megan.

"Welcome back, Gracie," Kris greets me as I enter the room and head toward my familiar space at the mirror.

"Hi, Kris," I return the blond's greeting. A quick glance around the room alerts me to some changes. I look quizzically at Kris.

"Megan's character got written off, so all her stuff is gone," Kris explains.

"That's too bad," I say, shocked that the character would have been eliminated.

"It's okay. Megan asked them to. She and her husband are trying to get pregnant."

"That makes much more sense. What about Danielle?"

"She's around somewhere."

Kris and I catch up on each other's lives, me regaling her with LA stories and she sharing set gossip I had missed.

"The boy gets a divorce and guess who shows up."

I roll my eyes. "Good to see you, too, Danielle," I greet her as she enters the room.

She smiles. "Seriously, the timing is rather fortuitous."

"Fortuitous?" Kris snorts. "Knock it off with the 50-cent vocab words."

Danielle tosses her red hair dismissively. "Can I help it if I'm more educated than you are?"

"It's true, then? Julian filed for divorce?" I attempt to ask this nonchalantly amidst their back and forth banter, but Kris and Danielle exchange a knowing glance.

"Yep, it's true."

They are clearly waiting for a response from me. "Hmm," is all I say.

"What are you going to do?" Danielle asks when it becomes obvious I am not going to respond further.

"I don't know," I sigh. "I'll figure that out when I see him."

"Good luck," Kris chimes in.

I am hyperaware of my surroundings as I dress in wardrobe, receive hair and makeup, and finally arrive on the set. No Julian yet.

"Is that little Gracie, returned to the fold?" I smile when I hear Richard Garcia's voice behind me. I turn to my "brother."

"Hey, Max," I respond with his character's name. He wraps me in a bear hug and spins me around. I shriek in delight.

"You're like a doll, you're so tiny," he says after putting me down. I punch him lightly on the arm.

"Only my brother can get away with saying that to me."

Richard and I sit on a nearby church pew (part of the wedding chapel set) to chat until Miranda Borden, the (still harried-looking) director arrives on set to begin shooting.

"Hello, everybody," Miranda greets the room. Spotting me, she adds, "Welcome back, Gracie." I nod an acknowledgment and she continues. "We're actually going to shoot somewhat in order today."

Everybody reacts in feigned shock and she smiles.

"We'll shoot the wedding rehearsal and wedding party dinner before lunch. Then, with almost the full cast, we'll shoot the wedding and the large group scenes of the reception after lunch. Let's roll."

With those words, the set jumps into motion. I barely have time to breathe, let alone think about a certain newly single beautiful soap star. All that changes when the director says…

"That's lunch, people."

I am instantly filled, not with thoughts of my scenes after lunch, but with the knowledge that Julian is in those wedding and reception scenes. I don't have any lines with him and right now it's a coin flip whether that is a good or bad thing.

"Hey, Janie," comes Richard's voice, again behind me.

"Yes, brother," I say, smiling as I turn to face him. It's funny how quickly a character name can sound so natural to the ears.

Richard has an uncertain look on his face and my smile falters. "He's here," is all he says.

"Thanks," I respond, to have a response. I smile to show him, it's okay, I can see Julian without falling apart or wanting to jump his bones. Maybe.

Without a clear reason, I try to postpone the inevitable by purposefully wandering during lunch and then, when it's time, preparing for the wedding scene. Eventually I find myself stationary on the wedding set, waiting for everything to begin.

I don't know how, exactly, but I can sense when Julian has entered the room. I know he's watching me from behind and I have to will myself not to find him, to seek out his face.

"Hey, Gracie," one of the production assistants calls as she passes by me.

"Hi, Amy," I return the greeting with a small wave. Oh, screw it. I scan the room until I find Julian. As I suspected, he is watching me. When our eyes meet, he smiles. Like one of Pavlov's dogs, I automatically return the smile and begin walking toward him. Seeing my motion, Julian, too, starts to walk. We meet halfway.

"Hi," he says softly, uncertainly.

"Hi," I respond, equally uncertain. And, so far, another scintillating conversation. "How have you been?" This is somewhat of an inane question to ask a man recently divorced.

He gives me his lopsided grin that I love. "It's been up and down. How have you been?"

"Great," I reply airily. "I've been in Los Angeles working on some projects."

"That's wonderful. Anything catch fire?"

"Nah," I admit. "But, they were fun to do."

"I'm sure." Julian's expression turns serious. "I missed you."

I can feel panicky fluttering in my chest. I was hurt so bad before; could it really be different this time? Yes, my internal voice hollers. The look on Julian's face tells me my response is taking a trifle long. "I missed you, too," I finally say. We're both silent for a minute. It's not quite awkward.

"I'd really like a chance to talk to you," Julian says. "Privately."

"Yeah?" The hustle and bustle around us goes up a notch, signaling lunch is almost over. I glance around. "When?"

"Neither of us is filming tomorrow." I raise an eyebrow. "Yes, I checked your schedule. How about lunch?"

"That would be nice."

"The place around the corner?"

"Perfect." And our timing could not have been more perfect to end the conversation, as Miranda walks on set.

"Everybody ready," the director announces, rather than asks. The activity in the room raises another notch.

"If we don't talk again today, I'll see you tomorrow," Julian tells me with a flash of his beautiful smile.

"I'll see you later," I respond.

We separate and head to our areas.

Staging a wedding with an entire cast is actually a lot more complicated than one might imagine, given the number of physical bodies present, the lighting requirements, and the plethora of camera shots of various pairs and groupings to capture the scene. Nevertheless, Miranda works her magic and we successfully shoot the wedding and large group scenes at the reception that had been her goal.

Unfortunately, the craziness of the afternoon and evening does not allow me another opportunity to speak with Julian. Still, I leave the studio at the end of the day with a skip in my step, excited and nervous about my lunch date tomorrow.

Will he want to try again, now that he's divorced, or will he want some space to recover from the emotional trauma?

CHAPTER THIRTY-FOUR

"How was your first day back?"

"It went well," I answer Jane, uncharacteristically circumspect. I walk to the kitchen to pour myself juice.

"Don't overwhelm me with details," she says sardonically from the living room.

I laugh. "Sorry. I think I'm still lost in my own thoughts. I almost missed my subway stop."

"That's pretty lost," she agrees. "Pray tell, what were you thinking about?"

"Pray tell?" I join her on the couch.

"I just watched a British period piece," Jane explains.

"Yep, that'll do it."

"So?"

"Right. I have a date tomorrow?"

"Who with?"

"Julian."

Jane's eyes widen. "That was fast. Tell me everything."

When I finish recounting my interlude with Julian, I sigh. "Am I over-thinking it?"

"Sure, but you like him. This is the equivalent of a second chance. You don't want to mess it up."

"Well put."

"Thanks. I try."

"What do you think?" I ask, not sure what I'm asking.

"I think you should go to lunch with Julian tomorrow. Be honest, but don't rush anything. You guys obviously made a connection before, but he is just getting out of a failed marriage."

"Good advice. You should write a column," I add.

"Smart ass."

"No, seriously. Thanks."

"You're welcome. Now tell me the Julian-unrelated gossip from the set."

"Yes, ma'am," I say with a mock salute.

"And, you've got great timing. The pizza should be here in about five minutes."

"Pizza? Sweet. Being on set again was great," I begin. Jane and I talk about this and that, most of it probably instantly forgettable. I even manage not to think about Julian at all. Or at least not much.

The next morning I find random activities to occupy my time until I can reasonably leave.

"You know you're going to be early," Jane points out needlessly.

"What if the trains are delayed?"

"That could happen," she agrees.

"I don't want to be late."

"Of course not," she agrees again.

"Quit being so agreeable," I tell her, sticking out my tongue. "You brought it up."

Jane smiles. "Have fun."

"Thanks." I return the smile.

I leave the apartment and head for the stairs. Exiting the building, I am struck by how sunny and beautiful the day is, though still cold, since spring is still a month or so away. Bundled in my jacket, I walk slowly, savoring the excitement. The subways are, of course, not delayed and I arrive at the restaurant nearly twenty minutes early. I decide to get a table anyway.

Pulling open the door and stepping inside, I break into a wide smile. I walk toward a booth in the back.

"You're early," Julian says in greeting.

"So are you," I point out, taking a seat opposite him.

"I didn't want to be late."

"Me, neither," I agree with a laugh.

The waitress arrives then and we both order water and vegetable paninis.

"How's your day?"

"Getting better and better," I respond without thinking. Slow down!

Julian smiles, laughter in his eyes. "I'm glad. It's good to see you again," he says, suddenly serious. "I missed you."

"I missed you, too. It was good to see you yesterday." Although heartfelt, the conversation is sounding inane (again) to my own ears.

"It was all I could do not to sweep you into my arms and kiss you yesterday," Julian continues. My nipples harden at the decidedly not-inane turn of the conversation.

"I would have liked that."

"Wanna get out of here?" He asks playfully, though his voice has become husky and his eyes liquid longing.

I close my eyes and savor the thought. My body may be screaming yes, but my mind is still warning me to slow it down. "As fabulous as that would be," I say upon opening my eyes, "shouldn't we, I don't know, talk first."

"I was only half-serious," he says with a slow, sensuous smile. "Talk is good, too."

"How are you doing? You know, with the divorce?" I ask tentatively.

"Despite Lydia's dishonesty, I had real feelings for her and the commitment we made." He pauses, gathering his thoughts. "I thought I loved her. I think I loved the idea of her as the mother of my child."

"I can't imagine how hard that must have been for you."

"When I found out she lied about the pregnancy, it forced me to reevaluate myself, her, and our relationship. Then I met you."

"Then you met me."

"It all happened so fast. I was still so mixed up in my own mind. I didn't know if I could trust my feelings. I didn't know if I liked you for you, or because you were this force of nature."

"Force of nature?" I smile at the description.

"I'd never met anyone like you."

"I wish I had known this before."

Julian gives me a questioning look.

"I didn't know if you'd really had feelings for me at all."

"Don't ever question that," Julian says earnestly. "When I said I needed time, it was genuinely so I could figure out what was best for me and for Lydia."

"Divorce? Did Lydia agree?"

"Not at first. We sat down together and had one of our only honest conversations. She admitted her dishonesty and I admitted that I didn't love her. It was painful but, in the end, we agreed that a divorce was the best option."

"And it had nothing to do with me," I venture. "Not to be egotistical." Julian smiles.

"I wouldn't say it had nothing to do with you," he begins. "Not the decision to divorce," he hurries to add, seeing my horrified expression. "You showed me what I would miss out on if I stayed with Lydia out of a misguided sense of loyalty or commitment. I didn't want that for either of us."

"And now?"

"I thought I would want more time to be sure, but the instant I saw you on set…" Julian trails off, shaking his head.

"What?"

"I knew."

"Knew what?"

"That I was addicted."

"To me?"

"To you. Hasn't anyone told you that you're addictive?"

"Not that I recall," I say with a laugh, then grow serious. "Addictions can become dangerous and out of control."

"Let's lose the analogy, then." Julian reaches across the table to take my hands in his. "My friends warned me not to scare you off, but I want to get everything out." I am silent while he takes a deep breath. "I think I loved you the first time I saw you." Yikes. "Getting to know you deepened those feelings." Rounding third and heading for home. "Being away from you was like torture." What else is there? "I won't go crazy and propose today, but that'll probably happen sooner rather than later." That's what else. And my friends thought I'd be the one rushing things. "Gracie?"

"Sorry," I say, smiling sweetly. "I was caught in my internal dialogue." I rub his fingers lightly with my own.

"Hearing voices?"

"Just my own," I respond to his teasing.

"What are they saying?"

"That this all seems too good to be true."

"Do you believe that?"

"No, I don't. I believe you. I believe *in* you. I believe in our feelings for each other. Though if you had proposed right now,

I can't promise I wouldn't have run out of the restaurant." My comment perceptibly lessens the intensity of the mood.

"I'm glad I restrained myself."

"Me, too." I rise, then, not breaking physical contact with Julian, and sit next to him on the other side of the booth. "Kiss me," I demand and he obliges. We kiss like lovers who have been separated by the ages, by continents, well, you get the idea.

"My mother is having a belated family dinner next weekend to celebrate my return to the city," I tell him when we finally separate. "Do you want to come?"

"Meet your family?"

"Yep."

"Absolutely."

We smile at each other like teenagers in love. I carry that feeling with me through the remainder of lunch, shooting the rest of the week, and pretty much everything I do until finally, it is Saturday. I know I'll be seeing Julian that night.

CHAPTER THIRTY-FIVE

"Are you kidding me?" The smile drops from my face and the words fly out of my mouth before I can even think. The blond leaning against my building straightens up, stubbing her cigarette out under her boot.

"Gracie?" There is something different about her tone, but I ignore it.

"I have nothing to say to you, Alicia," I respond brusquely and attempt to pass by her.

She tentatively reaches out a hand to stop me.

"Don't touch me," I hiss.

"Look, you have every right to be furious with me," Alicia White, crazy meth-head wife of my former lover, tries.

"Thanks for the permission," I respond acidly. I don't know why I am quite this agitated. I thought I had resolved my issues with her and her husband months ago. Maybe it's because she's intruding on my day with Julian.

"Please just give me five minutes," she cries desperately and a tone in her voice makes me pause.

"Five minutes," I tell her, not quite civilly.

"Thank you," she says so pitifully that I actually feel guilty for my attitude. Until I remember the guinea pig.

I give a slight nod of my head, signaling her that she can begin.

"I've been in rehab for the past two months," she says without preamble, reaching to light a new cigarette. "That's where I picked up this habit."

"That's one minute," I say as she takes a long drag on the cancer stick.

"I graduated last week," she continues. Graduated?

"Wait a minute," I interrupt. "Am I a step? Isn't there something about making amends?" I can't quite keep the sarcasm out of my voice, which either Alicia misses or chooses to ignore.

"My program wasn't a 12-step program," she explains, "but there is a similar idea about making things right with people you hurt."

"You're here to make things right?" I ask, still skeptical of her true motives, although she certainly seems genuine.

"Yes, Gracie. Please let me explain myself."

Against my better judgment and even though her five minutes had lapsed, I invite her up. "You might as well come up to the apartment," I tell her as I open the front door to the building.

"Really?" She's like an eager puppy looking for a treat but expecting the rolled up newspaper.

"Yes," I say with a sigh as she follows me in and we start up the stairs. "I'd better not be featured on the 11 o'clock news as a dead body," I say in all seriousness.

"As if they'd find the body," she responds offhandedly and I stop cold. "Kidding," she hurries to add, laughing nervously.

I stifle another sigh and continue up the stairs, wondering about my ongoing naiveté with people. Really, I'm just too much of an optimist. I can hear Jane inside the apartment as I unlock our front door.

"Hey, Gracie. Are you excited about-" Jane abruptly stops as my guest becomes visible to her behind me.

"Hey, Jane. Can you give us a minute?"

"Are you sure?" Jane's worry is palpable.

"Yeah," I respond wearily.

Jane rises from the couch. "I'll just be in the other room."

"Thanks," I say, touched by her concern for my welfare. Of course, if I'd quit doing crazy things, she'd have no reason to be concerned. I focus on the issue at hand.

"Please, have a seat," I indicate the couch as I lock the front door behind us without thinking. Oh, well, there goes my quick escape route. I take a seat on the chair and face Alicia on the couch.

Alicia looks uncertain.

"It's your party," I say, by way of encouragement. Then the dam breaks.

"Gracie, I am so, so sorry for everything I did. I was high when I did most of it, but not all of it, and that's no excuse anyway."

I am taken aback by the strength of her emotions and say nothing in response. Unfortunately, she interprets this as more of my cold behavior.

"Please, Gracie. Give me a chance to explain."

The pleading in her voice snaps me out of my…shock, I guess, and I hold up my hands in surrender. "Alicia, it's fine. Tell me what you want to say." I strive to sound more inviting and it works. Alicia visibly relaxes and when she speaks again, the anxious agitation is gone.

"I wanted to apologize for all of it. I sent the black roses. I also stole some of your mail one time, I don't know if you knew your mail had been taken." Her tone is questioning.

"The door left ajar and my roommate's missed bill made that pretty clear," I respond wryly.

Alicia's cheeks color slightly. "Of course." She stares at me, clearly wanting to say something else, but hesitant to do so. I remain silent, watching the internal struggle play out across her face. Finally, she sighs, almost imperceptibly. Looking down at her hands, clutched in her lap, she speaks.

"I sent the guinea pig." I can barely hear her, but I know what she said.

"Why?" I ask this without mirth or artifice, but because I genuinely want to know how someone could kill and dismember an innocent being to freak out someone you're mad at.

"I...I don't know," she stammers, still so softly as to be barely audible. She looks up at me with tears in her eyes.

"To kill a little animal," I begin, but she cuts me off.

"Kill?" She repeats, aghast. "I didn't kill the guinea pig."

Now I'm confused. "I don't understand," I tell her.

Alicia has gone white. "All this time you thought I killed Taylor."

"Taylor? Oh, the guinea pig," I answer myself, briefly confused again. "Didn't you?"

"Oh my God, no," she insists. "You must have a pretty low opinion of me to think I would, or even could, do such a thing."

"What else could I think?" I ask, almost helplessly.

"Of course," she agrees. "It would seem quite the coincidence that the guinea pig happened to die around the time I lost my marbles."

"Well, yeah," I say with a half-shrug.

"That is what happened, though. Taylor had been sick and one day, when I was h-h-high," Alicia stammers on the word, "I noticed she wasn't breathing. I couldn't detect a heartbeat when I touched her." Alicia's eyes are welling up again and I fight the urge in me to join her. "I must have stared at her for hours, willing her to wake up. Nothing. Then, for reasons I'll never know, I started thinking of you and your affair with my husband." I start to interject and she shakes her head. "Sorry, my husband's affair. Anyway, the next part is hazy, but I," quick intake of breath here, "cut her into pieces and brought her to your doorstep." Alicia is openly crying now. Despite my desire to remain mostly unmoved, I feel tears well in my eyes. Crap. "I don't know what I was thinking. One thought kept running through my mind. A pig for a pig."

Yep, that dried the tears in my eyes. "I'm a pig?"

"Of course not! That's just what my state of mind was back then." Alicia stops and looks at me expectantly.

"I don't know what to say," I admit. "You don't know how it felt, believing a deranged meth addict was out to get me."

Alicia looks down at her hands again. "I'm sorry."

I sigh. "I know. Thank you for coming here to acknowledge what you did."

"Thank you for letting me," she says, looking up again with a hopeful expression. "Can I ask you something?"

"Why stop now?" I respond with a half-smile.

"Can you forgive me?"

I take a long moment to truly consider the question. "Yes, I think I can," I answer. She smiles widely. Aren't I magnanimous?

"I'm so glad. I'm working hard to maintain my sobriety and be the best person I can be. Christopher and I even went to counseling," she continues shyly.

This I definitely don't care to hear about, but I feign interest. "Oh?"

"Yes, and I think it's helping."

"I'm so glad for you." I can't quite keep the sarcastic tone from my voice but thankfully, Alicia again misses it, or chooses to ignore it. She does, however, abruptly rise from her seat.

"I've taken up enough of your time," she says and begins heading for the door.

I jump to my feet, following. "I'm glad we had this talk," I say, for lack of anything better.

"Me, too." Then she's gone. I close the door slowly, throw the deadbolts, and turn around. Jane has come out of her bedroom and is standing there with eyes wide.

"You heard?"

"Every word. Damn."

"It's over."

That is the extent of our conversation about Alicia White. I hope I never see or hear from Alicia or Christopher again.

CHAPTER THIRTY-SIX

I am still feeling discombobulated a few hours later when Julian arrives at my door to accompany me to my mother's family dinner.

"What's the matter?" he asks immediately.

"You wouldn't believe me if I told you," I respond.

"Try me," he says with an encouraging smile.

I give Julian the abridged version of the Christopher and Alicia saga, while we grab a taxi to my parents' place in Brooklyn. With near perfect timing, the taxi pulls in front of their building as I conclude the story.

"You date married men?"

"I tell you all of that, and this is what you get out of it." I'm shaking my head while I open the taxi door.

"I don't know, that fact stood out to me," Julian teases.

"Gee, I wonder why?" I stand outside the taxi, waiting for Julian to slide out.

"It was one of the more salacious bits," he insists. We're standing outside the building, facing each other. I take his hand in mine.

"Forget it, goofball. Let's go in and meet the family." We begin walking.

"Do you think they'll like me?"

I give him a sidelong glance. "Of course they'll like you. They know I love you."

Julian gives my hand a tiny squeeze, but says nothing.

I open the door to my parents' brownstone, announcing our arrival. "We're here," I sing out.

"Gracie! Welcome back from Los Angeles!" My sister flies across the living room and nearly knocks me on my ass with her tackle disguised as a hug.

"Maria, it's good to see you." We disentangle from each other. I intend to introduce Julian but already the rest of the family is approaching.

"Graciella, you're home," my father says, also giving me quite a bear hug.

"Welcome back, Gracie," chimes in my brother with a normal hug that doesn't threaten to crush my bones.

"Graciella, my love." My mother has actually left the kitchen to greet me – during dinner preparations. I'm starting to feel special.

"Hey, guys, I missed you, too, but, dang, I wasn't gone that long."

"Language," my father automatically intones.

"Sorry," I say from habit rather than contriteness. I step away from Julian, so they can see him clearly, and finally get a chance to introduce him. He shakes hands with each, even my mother, as I introduce my family members.

"Julian, this is Maria, my sister who's the model."

"I can see why," Julian comments and Maria blushes.

"This is Anthony, my older brother. He's a firefighter."

"Nice to meet you. Thanks for all you do."

Anthony nods in appreciation.

"This is my mother, Annabella."

"You've raised a wonderful woman."

"Thank you," is all she says, but I can tell my mother's pleased by the comment.

"And Julian, this is my father, Tomas. He's a retired city worker."

"It's a pleasure to meet you, sir. I love your daughter. I will do my best to protect her and make her happy," Julian says during the extended handshake with my father.

"I can tell you are a good man," my father responds. I exchange a glance with mama over this comment. That's high praise coming from my father. Julian really said the right thing.

"Come in, come in and sit down," my mother encourages. We all walk the ten feet to the couch. "I have to go to the kitchen to finish dinner. Spinach ravioli with vermicelli in gravy." She has already left the room by the time she speaks the last word.

"Gravy?" Julian whispers. We've taken seats on a loveseat, appropriately enough I suppose.

"Marinara," I whisper back with a smile.

Three sets of eyeballs stare at us and I wait for the Inquisition to begin. Somewhat surprisingly, my brother opens with a zinger.

"Julian, are you going to cheat on Gracie?"

"Anthony!" I am shocked by his brazen opening. Julian takes my hand.

"Gracie, it's okay. No, Anthony, I'm not."

"Didn't you cheat on your first wife with Gracie?" Anthony continues in an argumentative tone. I shoot him a murderous look, but Julian answers as if asked about the weather.

"Did I meet and fall in love with your sister while I was still married? Yes. Did I have an affair? I don't believe so."

"You don't believe so?" The skepticism drips from my brother's mouth.

"Once I admitted to myself I had developed feelings for Gracie, I took a step back to reevaluate everything." Julian looks at me with an apologetic expression because he knows now how much that "reevaluation" hurt me. I smile reassuringly.

"What's to say you won't meet someone else and fall in love again?"

I can't believe how difficult Anthony is being. Thus far, my father and Maria seem content to sit back and watch the verbal exchange like a tennis match.

"The situation with my first wife was very different," Julian begins slowly.

"You don't really have to answer that," I interrupt.

Looking at my brother, Julian disagrees. "Yes, I do. I never had feelings for her like I do for Gracie." Maria smiles happily at me. I think she certainly approves of my new man.

Suddenly, Anthony breaks into a wide grin. "Not too bad, my man. You held your cool."

"Gee, brother, was that a test?" I ask dryly.

"Definitely."

I roll my eyes. "At least you passed," I say to Julian.

"Now that the test is over," Maria jumps in, "tell me what it's like being a famous soap star. And what Gracie's really like to work with." Anthony laughs and even papa cracks a smile at Maria's stars-in-her-eyes tone.

Julian indulges my sister and regales her with stories from the sets of our daytime drama and his brief movie career, until my mother pops her head in the living room.

"Dinner is ready."

"Thank God," I mutter under my breath, but my brother hears me.

"Do you think the conversation will be any different during dinner?" Anthony asks quietly as we move en masse into the kitchen.

"Anthony, are you seeing anyone?" I ask cheerfully, and loudly.

"Anthony, have you met a nice girl?" My mother asks hopefully in response and I smile widely.

"I'll get you for that," he responds softly, rolling his eyes at me. I guess the eye rolling is hereditary.

By now we are seated at the kitchen table and all eyes are on my brother, waiting for him to answer the question.

"Yes, as a matter of fact, I have." In books, people write about bedlam; that's what broke out in my parents' kitchen over my brother's remark.

"Who is she?"

"Where did you meet?"

"Is she from the neighborhood?"

"Is she Italian?"

The overlapping questions are asked — even mama has paused in bringing the food to the table. I jump up to help her finish while Anthony answers the barrage.

"Her name is Jasmine. We met at work. She's not from the neighborhood and she's not Italian. Was that all?" Anthony asks with mock exasperation. I can tell he's happy talking about his new love.

"I'm not Italian either," Julian quips. I nudge him to hush. Nobody notices his comment anyway. My brother with a girlfriend is big news.

"Tell us more," Maria urges.

"She's Egyptian. She's a translator for the NYPD. I met her on a case. We borrowed her services after a fire."

"Clearly, you liked what you saw," I tease, though in truth I couldn't be happier for my brother.

We eat the fabulous dinner my mother prepared while Anthony divulges everything he knows about his new girlfriend. She may not be Italian, but our mother certainly doesn't seem to care. When he's finished, Maria catches us up on her latest modeling news and our parents reveal (surprise, surprise) they've become more involved in the church, going to potluck dinners and volunteering on the community board. When the food is gone and everyone is finally talked out, Julian and I say our goodbyes.

"Thank you so much for the wonderful meal, Mrs. Corsini."

"Julian, call me Annabella."

"Annabella, then," he obliges.

"It's been a great pleasure meeting all of you. I truly feel like you've welcomed me with open arms." My mother beams with pleasure at the remark. "I'm sure I'll see you again soon."

"Maybe at a wedding?"

"Maria!" Oy, my family.

"I meant at Anthony's, Graciella. What did you think I meant?"

I choose to ignore her. "We have to go now. It's been lovely, as always." Julian and I walk to the door, my family trailing behind.

At the door, we exchange hugs all around.

"I like him," my father whispers.

"He's a keeper," my brother whispers.

"You look happy," my mother whispers.

"He's hot," Maria almost whispers.

"Thanks, guys," I say in a normal tone of voice.

And then, Julian and I are standing outside the building bathed in the white noise of the city. We walk toward the street.

"They liked me."

"Heard those whispered comments, did you?"

"Nobody in your family has mastered the art of the whisper."

I punch him playfully in the arm. "Including me?" I ask.

Julian only laughs as he hails a taxi. He opens the door. "My love."

"Thank you, sir," I say as I enter the cab and slide over to the far side.

"I liked them, too," he says after entering the taxi beside me and I snuggle against him.

"I'm glad." My eyes flutter, trying to stay open.

"My place?"

"Lead the way." I'm feeling pretty awake now.

Our night of lovemaking is beautiful and the perfect ending to the evening. It's like a storybook ending, if fairytales actually included the sex part of the romances they tell, anyway.

The next two weeks are filled with shooting *Heart's Home* and spending every available moment with Julian. Since we decided to truly be together, being apart is practically impossible.

And then the cold water of real life douses me when I arrive home after work to find Tommy Pullman on my proverbial doorstep. I wish people would quit doing that to me.

"Hello, Graciella Corsini," he greets me in a singsong voice the crazy homeless usually employ.

"Hi, Tommy," I return the greeting warily.

"Bet you'd like to know why I'm here." He doesn't seem high, but something is... off.

"If you'd care to tell me."

"I'm cleaning house." Up goes the crazy factor.

"What does that mean, Tommy?" I am trying to respond to him in the most unthreatening manner possible, as though he is a wild beast who may snap and bite off my head at any moment.

"People are talking."

"Hmm, huh." I make small noncommittal noises. Meanwhile, I'm trying to plan my escape from this way-weird conversation. The fear has begun building inside of me.

"I have to stop the talking."

Oh, good, he's hearing voices. Tommy's eyes widen and I wonder if I was wrong about him using something. Heroin, cocaine maybe? He is clearly deranged, but seems sober somehow. But what do I know?

"How?"

Tommy's eyes now narrow to slits and he drags one finger across his throat. I recognize the universal sign and feel the blood drain from my face. We stare at each other for a few long seconds.

"First that annoying lawyer," he finally continues. The assistant district attorney! He's the one who killed him? As though reading my mind, he continues. "Yep, I did it. I framed Nicky for it."

Oh God, oh God, this can't be good that he's telling me this. I can sense my mortal danger edging closer and closer to an unseen red line. Before I can pull a coherent thought from my petrified brain, Tommy continues again.

"That's okay, though, because I took care of Nicky."

"You took care of Rossini?" I half-ask, half-confirm.

"If he hasn't been found yet, he soon will be," Tommy tells me gleefully.

I make a small, strangled noise in my throat. That's two murders he's now confessed to!

"How did you know Nicky's last name?" The question is asked rather conversationally, belying the menace I sense beneath.

"Wha-what?" I stammer my response. I have never been so scared in my life. I feel like ice water has been poured down my spine and every hair on my body is standing at terrified attention. I'm like a deer caught in the headlights of Tommy's deadeye stare.

"How did you know Nicky's last name?" He repeats the question, reinforcing, rather effectively, his intimidating stance, by taking a step toward me. I automatically take a step back and his lips form a lazy smile.

My mind finally starts working again. "Newspaper," I blurt out.

"What?" The eyes have narrowed again.

"I saw Nicky's last name in the newspaper after ADA Myers' murder," I say slowly and clearly, hoping this tames the wild beast hinting to emerge. And, miraculously, it seems to.

Tommy laughs and his facial muscles relax. He appears almost normal again. Almost.

"Of course you did. It was in the papers when they arrested poor Nicky. You should have seen his look of surprise when they arrested him." Tommy seems so normal now, we could be having a conversation about sports, or even the weather. "He was even more surprised when I slit his throat." Except for that, I suppose.

Although I am still scared, the bizarreness of our exchange becomes too much. "What do you want, Tommy? Are you here to kill me?" I can't believe I'm being this brazen with a confessed killer, but honestly I may die of fright if this is extended too much.

Tommy's eyes widen comically. They're quite expressive today, I must say. "Why would I kill you, Gracie? I like you. I just wanted to let you know I had taken care of some things."

"That's good," I say slowly, completely out of my element in terms of holding up my end of the wacky conversation.

"We understand each other," Tommy asserts rather than queries and I merely nod.

What words would even be appropriate?

And, just like that, he lopes off in the opposite direction from which I'd come.

My knees shake like they're about to collapse and it is all I can manage to open the door to the building, drag my butt up the stairs, and bang into the apartment. I quickly lock every lock on the door before actually collapsing on the couch before

Jane's astonished eyes. I have never been so rattled, even with all that has come before.

"What's the matter, Gracie? You look like you've seen a ghost."

"I almost did. Mine."

"What?!"

I quickly repeat the entire conversation with Tommy to Jane and she is quite naturally horrified.

"What do I do?"

"Are you kidding? Call the police."

"But he basically just told me he's going to leave me alone." I was already planning to call Aliana Gregson, my favorite lawyer in the district attorney's office. I just need someone to convince me I am making the right decision.

"Yes, but he's crazy," Jane says, with a note of hysteria in her voice. "He's killed two people out of what sounds like straight up paranoia. What happens when he decides you're talking about him?"

"He kills me," I say woodenly.

"Right. He kills —" Jane stops and eyes me. "You've already decided to call, haven't you?"

"Yes, but thanks for providing my argument." I roll over onto my stomach and close my eyes. "I'll call in the morning."

Jane rubs my hair as she passes me, heading for the kitchen. "I think that's reasonable. Do you want some ice cream?"

I raise my head. "Oh, definitely."

CHAPTER THIRTY-SEVEN

The next morning dawns far too beautiful for phone calls about murders, but I resist the highly tempting urge to stick my head in the sand and forget all about Tommy and his threats. After a deliberately leisurely shower and breakfast, I give up avoiding and dial Aliana Gregson's office number. I skip the social niceties after the receptionist transfers my call.

"Tommy Pullman killed Leonard Myers and Nicholas Rossini," I declare dramatically.

"Gracie Corsini? Is that you? How did you know Rossini was dead? That information hasn't been released yet." Lawyers are the greatest at the rapid-fire delivery of questions that do not allow you a chance to actually answer any.

"Yes, this is Gracie Corsini. I know Rossini is dead because Tommy Pullman told me," I take a deep breath, "when he confessed to the murder."

"What?" I can hear the confusion in the lawyer's voice. "Why don't you start at the beginning?"

I oblige and recount, as close to verbatim as I can, the conversation I had with Thomas Pullman, mobster extraordinaire, the night before. When I finish, I wait for Ms. Gregson's response.

"A male body washed up in the harbor only two days ago. We tentatively identified it as Nicholas Rossini, although official identification is pending." Ms. Gregson confirms what I already knew, her voice taking on a familiar no-nonsense, all-business tone.

"Great," I say wearily, already exhausted by the conversation and its implications. I think part of me had secretly been hoping he hallucinated that he committed these murders.

"Thomas Pullman confessed to the murders of Leonard Myers and Nicholas Rossini." As Ms. Gregson appears to be thinking aloud, I offer no comment. "Would you be willing to testify to the content of the conversation?"

"Isn't that hearsay or something?" Please?

"No, not quite," she answers, and I can hear the smile in her voice. Gee, I'm glad my lack of knowledge of the law amuses her.

"I'm right back in the middle of everything again."

"It would seem that way," she agrees.

"When will you arrest him?"

The long pause following my question alerts me to the fact that I am not going to like her answer.

"Not yet."

Nope, didn't like it. "When?"

"First, we have to confirm that Rossini is the body that we have down in the morgue."

"How long will that take?" I note a petulant tone creeping into my voice and try to contain it. "I just want this to end."

"I know you do," Ms. Gregson empathizes. "Now that we have a case to build against a specific defendant, I can put a rush on the identification. He should be arrested within a couple of days," she hurries to add before I can ask again.

I breathe a sigh of relief. I can make it a couple of days without developing an ulcer from the anxiety, or ending up an unidentified female body in the harbor, if Tommy finds out I'm testifying against him (again) before they can arrest him.

"Thank you," is all I say.

"Hang in there, Gracie. I think we can finally see the light at the end of the tunnel."

"I hope so."

We end the conversation and no sooner do I disconnect the call that I hear the beep signifying a text message. I smile when I see that it's from Julian.

"Heading to set. Still on for lunch Friday at park? Meet at fountain?"

Even though I know he's probably already turned off his cell phone, I immediately text him back.

"Yes to Friday at the fountain. Have fun shooting. Miss you!"

CHAPTER THIRTY-EIGHT

The next couple of days pass in a blur. I'm not shooting, but honestly could not say what I did with my time. I don't recall leaving the apartment much, if at all. It's hard to feel motivated to leave when a crazy murderer may just decide to add you to his "to clean house" list. Now, however, it's Friday, and I'm on my way to the park to meet Julian for lunch. I never did hear from Aliana Gregson that Thomas Pullman was arrested, so when my phone rings and I see that it's her office, I am sorely tempted to answer. But, I don't.

"She'll either tell me he's been arrested or give me an excuse why not," I say aloud, possibly frightening the pedestrians around me. Although, this being New York City, they probably didn't even notice! I just want one day free from dead bodies, mobsters, and veiled threats of bodily harm. Is that really too much to ask?

Apparently so, I discover, when I arrive early at the fountain. Imagine my shock and dismay when I turn around at a tapping on my shoulder and see, not the love of my life, Julian, but Tommy Pullman. The mobster who is supposed to be in jail.

I can immediately see that this time he is definitely high. His eyes are dilated to the size of saucers and he has that goofy "my brain isn't functioning right" look on his face. Tread with caution, my brain screams at me. I say nothing, deciding to let him lead this dance.

"Hello, Graciella Corsini," he greets me brightly.

"Hello, Thomas Pullman," I mirror, and immediately regret.

His eyes narrow. "Are you mocking me?"

"Of course not," I rush to convince. Ah, here comes the all-too-familiar rush of fear.

"Did we, or did we not, have a conversation the other day?"

"We did." Keeping my side of the conversation minimal seems like a good idea.

"What was the content of that conversation?"

Not sure what he wants me to say, I stare up at the sky as if pondering the question. In truth, I am hoping for a divinely-inspired lightning bolt. Alas, one is not forthcoming and my gaze returns to match his.

"We talked about my killing two people," Tommy says slowly, as if I am a moron. "Ringing any bells?"

"Yes," I whisper. Tendrils of fear continue snaking their way through me.

"Why would you go to the police?"

"Who says I went to the police?" Incredibly my voice sounds confident since, technically speaking, I didn't go to the police. This is a distinction I doubt will impress.

Tommy looks at me sadly. "I'm disappointed, Gracie. I thought we understood each other."

"We did. We do." I try for sincerity.

"Then why was I arrested yesterday?" Tommy asks, shaking his head still, like a disappointed father.

I shrug, but say nothing.

Mistake.

Tommy reaches into his jacket pocket and pulls out a gun. What kind? A really big black one.

Waving the gun around, Tommy begins a diatribe. I am dimly aware of hearing screaming around us. It's lunchtime; Central Park is crowded.

"How could you do this to me, Gracie? I trusted you. We had an understanding." Every sentence is punctuated by a violent gesture toward me with the gun. I manage not to step backward, just barely, sensing he would not react well. Fear incapacitates, anyway, so movement seems unlikely. Although, thus far, our conversation is going swimmingly, I must say.

I try to speak in the tone I've heard Oprah and Dr. Phil use with upset guests. "I understand that you're upset with me, but, please, let's talk about this."

"Talk? Now you want to talk?" If it's possible, he looks even more deranged than at the start of our conversation.

"Yes, I do. Hey, wait," I interrupt myself. "You were arrested?"

"As if you didn't know," he responds snidely. His eyes widen in understanding and he gives me a twisted smile. "You want to know how I'm out if I was arrested yesterday." I say nothing, wishing now I had answered Aliana Gregson's call. "In a word – bail."

"You got bail on two murders," I squeak out.

"Guess keeping that fancy, overpaid suit on retainer paid off."

"Guess so," I agree faintly. He won't have to kill me – the fear is going to.

"Don't be too mad at the district attorneys though," he consoles me. "They didn't say your name in court."

"No?" A flicker of hope rises that I can talk my way out of this situation. Out of the corner of my eye, I think I see Julian approaching. I deliberately don't look in his direction. No need to give Tommy another target while I wait for the police to arrive. Where the hell are they?!

"I'm not stupid, you know. You're the only one I confessed to," his voice rises considerably, "so I know it was you." He has resumed waving the gun at me.

I sense movement and am irresistibly drawn to look. I see Julian, closer than he was before. But, I was right. Tommy focuses his attention on Julian, who looks terrified on my behalf.

"The boyfriend?" He's watching Julian.

"Yes." I decide lying seems like a bad idea.

"Let's see how much he likes this." I'm watching Julian, too, and can see by his expression that something bad is about to happen. Before I can fully turn my head to face Tommy – SMASH – he slams the butt of his gun into my cheek. The pain is instantaneous and incredible. I feel like my cheek has exploded. While still comprehending I've been hit, I realize I've lost my balance and am falling backward.

The world is already fading as I fall. I think I hear Julian calling my name. Tommy's satisfied – no, smug – look is the last thing I see before I hit the ground, my head bouncing off the pavement.

And the world goes black.

CHAPTER THIRTY-NINE

I feel someone holding my head. "Please, wake up." Julian's voice, as if through a fog. I regain consciousness. I open my eyes and fix on his face.

"Hey there, stranger."

"Hey there, yourself. I thought I lost you."

"I'd never let you off that easy." I reach a hand to his face, wiping away the tears he had not realized he was crying.

Medical personnel try to come between us, to check me over, but I wave them away. "I'm fine, honestly. I just have a bitch of a headache."

I hesitantly rise from the ground, Julian scrambling to get up with me, holding my hands tightly. "Tommy?"

"Arrested. The police grabbed him the moment you fell and he was distracted."

"Thank God." I close my eyes briefly, feeling nauseous from the pain in my head.

Maybe I will let the paramedics check me over. When I give the signal, they rush in, shining a pen light in my face, asking questions. Eventually satisfied I'm not in imminent danger of death, they leave with my promise to get a head scan that very afternoon.

As I look into his face after the paramedics have gone, Julian's eyes change and he releases my hands. "What? What's the matter?" I ask.

Without a word, Julian drops to one knee, his hand reaching into his coat pocket. My eyes widen. What is he doing?

"I love you more than I ever thought it was possible to love another person. I want to spend the rest of my life with you."

I cry like a girl when Julian pulls a tiny jeweler's box from his pocket, opening it to reveal a small platinum band with an amethyst, surrounded by a spray of diamonds.

"Will you marry me?"

"How long have you had that?"

"Since the week I met you."

I look at him incredulously. "You have not."

"Yes, I have. I thought I was crazy at the time, with everything so undecided, but something in me told me to get it. I even have the receipt to prove it, if required."

"No. Proof isn't required," I reply, laughing. "You are so amazing."

"Yes, I know," Julian agrees with a smile. "You still haven't answered my question." I realize Julian is still on bended knee, holding out the ring. "Will you marry me?"

"Yes, yes, yes. Of course I will," I whisper, pulling Julian back to his feet and embracing him tightly. "I love you so much."

We kiss passionately as the crowd gathered around us begins clapping. I pull back from Julian and look up at him mischievously.

"What is that look for?" Julian asks with a smile in his voice.

"Turn around and find out."

As soon as Julian turns around, I jump onto his back. "Piggyback ride?"

"Naturally," Julian responds, as he walks toward the edge of the park and the rest of our lives together. "Any time you want."

EPILOGUE

Bright lights shine on Julian and me as we take our seats across from the latest blond bombshell (I believe she said her name is Brooke) to host *Entertainment Tonight*. She smiles her practiced smile, showing the perfect amount of teeth and gums. This is a woman who knows how she looks on television.

"Welcome back, everyone," Brooke directs her address to the camera. "I'm sitting down with those elusive daytime drama lovebirds, Julian McNamara and Graciella Corsini, to ask them about their fairytale romance."

She pauses and turns toward us. "Welcome, Julian, Graciella."

"Thank you," we reply in unison. Oh, goodness, I hope we won't come across like one of those irritating attached-at-the-hips couples.

"Of course, we've all read the stories in the tabloids. Why don't you tell me how the two of you met?"

Julian defers to me to answer the question and I begin at the beginning so to speak, though I know to speak in sound-bite size sentences and keep it brief.

"I asked him if he thought he could just be friends with me and he said yes," I say at the end of the tale.

"Boy, was I wrong!" Julian exclaims before squeezing my hand.

Brooke smiles. "Your story has it all – famous people, intrigue, and a happy ending. Your life would make a terrific movie."

Or a novel! And so it has.

THANK YOU!

Thank you so much for supporting my work and reading this book. I truly hope you enjoyed reading it as much as I did writing it.

If you liked the book, please consider leaving a review.

Just a few lines would be great. Reviews are not only the highest compliment you can pay to an author, they also help other readers discover and make more informed choices about purchasing books in a crowded online space. Thank you so much in advance.

If you didn't like the book or have concerns,
please email me directly at
hlsilvio@yahoo.com

ABOUT THE AUTHOR

Heather has written fiction and nonfiction; she is also an actress and licensed psychologist. When she isn't working, she channels her inner flapper as a 1920s jazz and blues singer. She lives in Las Vegas with her wonderful husband Sidney and their goofy cat Snowball.

Visit http://www.heathersilvio.com for more information and to sign up for her New Releases and Appearances Newsletter

www.ingramcontent.com/pod-product-compliance
Lightning Source LLC
Chambersburg PA
CBHW022356110726
47902CB00002BA/310